Martin Berry **The**
SAPPHIRE CRYSTAL

After finding they have special powers, two young friends are spirited away to a world of small green beings – and soon realise that the fate of their world, and our own, is in their hands.

Martin Berry

The SAPPHIRE CRYSTAL

After finding they have special powers, two young friends are spirited away to a world of small green beings – and soon realise that the fate of their world, and our own, is in their hands.

MEREO
Cirencester

Mereo Books

1A The Wool Market Dyer Street Cirencester Gloucestershire GL7 2PR
An imprint of Memoirs Publishing www.mereobooks.com

The Sapphire Crystal: 978-1-86151-733-3

First published in Great Britain in 2016
by Mereo Books, an imprint of Memoirs Publishing

The address for Memoirs Publishing Group Limited can be found at
www.memoirspublishing.com

The Memoirs Publishing Group Ltd Reg. No. 7834348

The Memoirs Publishing Group supports both The Forest Stewardship Council® (FSC®) and the PEFC® leading international forest-certification organisations. Our books carrying both the FSC label and the PEFC® and are printed on FSC®-certified paper. FSC® is the only forest-certification scheme supported by the leading environmental organisations including Greenpeace. Our paper procurement policy can be found at www.memoirspublishing.com/environment

Typeset in 13/20pt Century Schoolbook
by Wiltshire Associates Publisher Services Ltd. Printed and bound in Great Britain by Printondemand-Worldwide, Peterborough PE2 6XD

1

The small window at the side of Number One Partridge Way was overgrown with ivy, and although a late summer sun had pushed through the morning mist outside, inside the cupboard Melina could barely see her hands in front of her. She was floating in the air, close to the ceiling with the lightshade hanging down a few inches away from her middle. The cupboard was short from front to back, the same width as the stairs above, and to fit in she had to float on her side, with her knees pulled in towards her chest.

Melina found floating in the air effortless. All she had to do was think about getting away and being very light and she would drift gently up into the air. It was a peculiar sensation, a little unnerving, especially with it being so dark.

The house was very quiet. Every now and then she could hear her mother moving about on the floorboards upstairs. The spare room needed redecorating and her mother had taken time off at the hospital, where she worked as a pharmacist, to make a start on it. The rest of the family were out. Her father had gone to work. He worked in a bank in London and wouldn't be back until after tea. Lastly there was Joe, her younger brother, who'd gone to a friend's house for a birthday sleepover. Joe was probably the main reason the house was so quiet, because when he was there, he made most of the noise. Sometimes when he left the house, slamming the door behind him, she thought she could practically hear the house breathe a sigh of relief, safe in the knowledge that it was to get a break from the chaos and hullabaloo that seemed to surround its youngest occupant. Melina was glad Joe was out. They weren't supposed to go inside the cupboard, and if he'd seen her going in, he would probably have told on her.

Something brushed her cheek, and she discovered that some of her hair had fallen out of her scrunchie. Her hair was ginger, and almost waist length. It was hanging down below her, giving her away, so she gathered it up and tucked it back into the scrunchie. Her nose began to itch and prickle inside, and she thought she was going to sneeze, but after pinching it for a while, the feeling went away.

As her eyes grew more accustomed to the dark, she saw daylight creeping under the door. The pale lampshade came into view, and then the sloping side wall, which was covered in stripy wallpaper. If she squinted she could just make out the large cardboard box down on the floor where she'd left her trainers. She'd taken them off in case they marked the walls, and then hidden them inside, so that Lisa wouldn't find them.

****

"Forty-nine... fifty... COMING READY OR NOT!" yelled Lisa, before taking off across the kitchen, down the hall and into the living room, rucking up the rug near the front door and sending it sailing across the polished wooden floor. The living room was bright, with sunlight streaming through the patio doors, making the beige carpet in front of them glow. She started to search, checking the space at the other end of the settee next to the radiator, where she'd found Melina before. Next, she tried looking behind the armchair. But she had no luck there either.

Moving to the front window, she looked behind the curtains. It wasn't the easiest place to hide, as she'd found out herself from painful experience, perched on the hard windowsill with knees folded up, waiting, and after a while, wishing to be found.

"Nope, not there either," muttered Lisa.

She tried the dining room, her light brown ponytail brushing the floor as she bent down next to the dining table to look under the sideboard. Still nothing. She glanced about the room, but she couldn't see any more hiding places. "She must be upstairs," she muttered to herself. But after a thorough search, there was no sign of her up there either.

"This is ridiculous," grumbled Lisa, plonking herself down on the stairs. "She's got to be somewhere."

Tapping came from somewhere nearby. Tap... tap... tap... She shuffled down a few steps, trying to work out where it was coming from. Tap... tap... tap...

It appeared to be coming from under the stairs. In a flash of inspiration, she knew where Melina was hiding. She jumped to her feet and ran down the stairs, taking them two at a time. Skidding to a stop at the door to the under-stairs cupboard, she pulled on the handle, and the door jerked open with a loud click. She stepped inside, flicked on the light, and scanned the cupboard for any likely hiding places. The roof sloped down towards the floor on one side, and there was a large cardboard box sitting on the floor underneath. Lisa wondered if Melina was hiding behind it, and crouched down to take a look. But she was disappointed once more, as apart from a few old paint tins and a roll of carpet, the space was empty. There didn't appear to be anywhere else for Melina to hide, so she turned the light off, and came back out of the cupboard.

She was about to close the door when she heard a giggle. Thinking she might have missed something, she reopened it, and stepped back inside.

"ACHOO!"

Lisa nearly jumped out of her skin. The sneeze had come from above her. Looking up, she saw a pair of stockinged feet, then, craning her head back further, she saw

Melina grinning down at her.

"Oh! You gave me a heck of a fright," said Lisa.

"Sorry," said Melina. "It just came out."

"However did you get up there?" asked Lisa crossly.

Once found, Melina had planned to take her hands away from the wall and show Lisa her power. She'd replayed the moment over and over in her head, picturing the look of amazement on Lisa's face as she floated magically in the air above her. But now Lisa was in a bad mood, and it didn't feel like the right time to share it with her.

"I... climbed up," said Melina.

"Well come down!" snapped Lisa.

"All right. But you'll need to shut the door first, so... I can use it to get down."

A couple of minutes later the door opened and Melina appeared, looking a little sheepish. Her mother called down from upstairs, "I hope you're not in that cupboard, Melina?"

"No, Mum, we're in the hall," answered Melina. Which she reasoned was sort of true, because that was where she was now.

They moved into the living room. "So that's why you wanted to play hide and seek again, so you could make me jump," complained Lisa.

"No. Sorry I didn't mean to do that. That sneeze just came out. I must have knocked down some dust."

They were sitting on the sofa looking out of the patio door into the garden.

"Yes, well all right. But, I still don't see how you got up there."

"I told you, I climbed."

"But you were so high up. And anyway, there was nothing to get hold of…"

"How's Floss?" asked Melina, cutting her off in mid-sentence.

She'd spotted a framed photograph of Lisa with Floss. Floss was Lisa's pet rabbit, and she knew that if anything was going to take Lisa's mind off what had just happened, it would be her.

"What?" asked Lisa incredulously.

"Little Flossy, how is she?"

"She's fine. Why?"

"Let's go and see her."

"What, now?"

"Yes, come on," said Melina, hopping up from the sofa. As she opened the front door, she called out to her mother, "I'm just going round to Lisa's, Mum."

"OK, but don't forget lunch will be about two," came Mrs Fielding's reply.

Melina lived on the corner of Partridge Way, with Lisa living next door. She was twelve, a year older than Lisa. They'd known each other since they were small. Shortly after Lisa had moved in, Melina had spotted her in the back garden. She'd been crying, and Melina had pulled faces at her through the fence, and made her laugh.

Floss's hutch was in the back garden at the corner of the patio. It had two levels with a run at the bottom, and a hutch on top, with a small ramp in between the two. Floss was at the bottom, hopping up and down along the front of the run excitedly.

"Can we take her for a walk?" asked Melina.

"OK," said Lisa, "I'll get her harness. I think it's in the shed."

They lifted the lid off the run to get to her. Floss however had other ideas, and ran up the ramp and into the cupboard at the end of her hutch, thumping her back feet down loudly on the wooden floor.

"She doesn't seem very keen," said Melina.

"Oh, don't worry, she always does that. She'll be fine once we get her out."

On opening the door to the cupboard they found Floss sitting hunched up, her white rear end pointing towards them. Before she could bolt again Lisa quickly grabbed hold of her with both hands, lifted her out and put her down on top of the hutch. Melina then held her by the scruff while Lisa buckled her into her harness.

"There, there. See there's nothing to be

afraid of," said Melina, stroking one of Floss's long floppy snowy white ears as Lisa clipped on her lead.

Lisa picked her up and carried her over to the edge of the lawn, then put her down again. Floss set off across the grass with small, hesitant hops. She stopped a few feet away and started to wash her face, licking each fluffy white paw in turn and rubbing it against her whiskers, finishing off using both paws at the same time.

"Ah, I love it when she does that," said Melina. "She looks so sweet."

"Here, you take her," said Lisa, offering Melina the lead. Melina reached over to take it, and had almost got hold of it, when Floss took off, pulling it from her fingers.

"Why didn't you keep hold of it?" shouted Lisa angrily.

"I couldn't. She moved too fast."

The garden was split in two, with a rockery in the middle, and a vegetable patch at the bottom. Floss hopped to a stop just short of the rockery and started to nibble at a patch of clover in the grass.

They crept up slowly towards her, so as not to scare her off.

"You stop her running that way, and I'll come in from this side and try and catch her," said Lisa.

Floss continued eating, watching them warily. Lisa waited for a moment when she thought she might be off her guard, and then reached out to grab her. She came close to catching her, but at the last moment Floss leapt up backwards away from her grasp. She took off back up the garden, running down the path at the side of the garage, heading towards the side of the house and the drive.

"Oh no, we're going to lose her!" cried Lisa.

At that moment Mrs Wendell came out of the back door.

"MUM, CATCH HER!" shouted Lisa, running down the path, with Melina following closely behind. Her mother looked down, saw Floss and stuck her foot out, blocking her way.

"Oh no you don't," she said.

Floss turned and tried to make a break for the gap between the fence and the side of the garage, but found another foot blocking her way. This time it was Lisa's. After a few more attempted escapes they managed to persuade her to go back to her hutch. She stood up on her back legs with her front paws on the wire mesh of her run, hesitated for a second, and then jumped back inside, landing with a back foot in her water bowl. Lisa quickly put the lid back on top.

"You nearly lost her that time," said Mrs Wendell, joining them.

"Yeah, sorry she just slipped out of our fingers. Didn't she Melina?"

"Well try to be more careful," said her mother.

After Lisa's mother had gone back indoors the two of them stood watching Floss. She seemed to have forgotten her little escapade, and was sitting in her sawdust tray on the other side of the run, cleaning herself. They moved around and knelt down to get closer to her.

"She's okay isn't she?" asked Melina.

"Yeah, I think so," answered Lisa.

It was then that Melina noticed that the bottom of the run was blackened and burnt.

"What happened there?" asked Melina.

"Oh that. It caught fire."

"What! How?"

"I'm not sure really. I was putting sawdust down for her, and spilt some down there. I was sweeping it up, and it just burst into flames."

"But where did the fire come from?"

"That's the thing, I don't know. It just came out of nowhere. I managed to put it out with the watering can."

"Floss was okay though?"

"Yeah, she was up in the top bit."

Melina looked at her watch, and saw it had gone two o'clock. "Listen, I'd better be going. "But I was wondering if you fancied going on a bike ride tomorrow? We could go over to Gatehampton, to see the lock."

"That's an awful long way," moaned Lisa.

"Oh go on. We haven't been there for ages."

"Well, okay. But I'm not going if it's raining. I hate cycling in the rain."

2

Melina was sitting sideways at the kitchen table, watching her mother cooking sausages in a frying pan on the cooker. They were spitting violently.

"We're thinking we might bike over to Gatehampton tomorrow," said Melina.

"To the lock?"

"Yes."

"Well stay well behind the barrier," said Mrs Fielding, turning the knob on the front of the cooker down to lower the heat. "And remember you haven't been very far on your new bike yet, so don't overdo it, or you'll end up saddle sore. Oh, while I'm thinking about it, we're planning on going into town tomorrow, so we could get Joe's present for you. His birthday's only a little over a week away now you know. So we haven't got long. Has he told you what he wants yet?"

"He said he wants that Bad Lands game they keep advertising on TV," said Melina. "But I asked around, and it seems everywhere's sold out."

"Well, I'll see if we can get it tomorrow," said her mother. "And if we can't, you'll just have to get him something else." She picked up the frying pan and tipped the sausages onto a plate she'd been keeping warm under the grill. "Go and tell your father dinner's ready."

"OK," said Melina.

Her father had been restoring an old sports car since as far back as she could remember. She used to help him when she was younger, sitting next to the toolbox and passing him tools. She often wondered if he would ever finish it, as he was such a perfectionist, working on every part until it looked like new. It had recently come back from being resprayed, and the racing green paint on the bodywork was gleaming.

As she entered the garage, she could hear him cussing.

"Are you all right under there?" asked Melina, looking over the top of the windscreen. He was lying across the passenger seat with his head half way under the dashboard, with a torch in his mouth.

"Yeah, just about," he said, without taking the torch out of his mouth. "These wires are a pig to do under here." This actually came out as "air gust agout ees ires arr a kig koo goo ungher ear."

This wasn't a problem for Melina, as she'd long since learnt to translate the unusual language of Torch-in-Mouth and understood every word.

"Mum says dinner's nearly ready," said Melina.

"ell urr irylle eee airr ingh a initt," he replied.

That night Melina couldn't get to sleep, and as she lay there her mind drifted back to the time when her mysterious power had first made its presence felt. It had been several months before at school during a PE lesson. It had been a Thursday, and as usual for a Thursday the class had been divided into groups, each group doing a different activity – running on the track, throwing the discus, putting the shot, high jump or long jump. Her group had been assigned the long jump. Running down the runway towards the sandpit, everything had seemed quite normal. It was after she'd reached the jump board that things got weird. As she'd leapt from the board she'd felt an unusual tingling in her legs, followed by a strange feeling of weightlessness, as if something powerful had been lifting her up, helping her into the air. The jump had seemed effortless, and she'd cleared the sandpit with ease before somersaulting to a stop in the grass at the other side.

A few of the girls in her group had come up to her and quizzed her about it, and she'd told them it was just a fluke, and that she wouldn't be able to do it again, but they hadn't seemed very convinced. Luckily, Mrs Handley, their teacher, had been supervising the shotput, and had had her back towards them, so she had been oblivious to it all.

Over the months that followed the tingling in Melina's legs gradually disappeared, but the strange power continued to grow. It soon grew so powerful that it could lift her off her feet without her doing anything at all, and there had been several occasions when she'd been forced to grab hold of something to stop herself from floating into the air. She had been getting increasingly concerned that if it continued to grow more powerful, someone might see her doing it. But then suddenly, everything changed, and she found that she had gained control of it, and become its master. From that moment on she no longer needed to worry about anyone seeing it, because she was in command.

3

The following day Melina collected her bike from the garage and wheeled it round to Lisa's. Walking up Lisa's drive, she could hear her friend banging about in the garden shed and grumbling to herself. After propping her bike up against the side of the house she called out to her, "Hang on Lisa, I'll give you a hand".

As she entered the shed she saw Lisa tugging at the back wheel of her own bike, trying to pull it out from under a blue tarpaulin. The tarpaulin slid off onto the ground, to reveal some old garden chair cushions and various other things, including an old orange garden hose, that seemed to have coiled itself around the frame like some evil bike-eating serpent.

"I wish people wouldn't put things on top of it," said Lisa.

They managed to disentangle it, and then found the tyres were flat. Lisa's pump was nowhere to be found, so they used Melina's, and after pumping up the tyres, they were ready to go.

"I've put a bottle of juice in your saddle bag," said Lisa's mother as they climbed on to their bikes. "And make sure you're back here by one for lunch. Have you got your phone?"

"Yes, yes it's in my pocket," sang Lisa, cheekily.

"Good," said her mother, scowling at her.

"Right we're off then. Bye," said Lisa pushing down hard on her pedals, keen to get away before her mother thought of something else that she might have forgotten.

Partridge Way was at the edge of the

Castle Field estate, and it was only a short ride up to the main road.

"This is great, isn't it?" said Melina, as she stopped at the junction, shortly before Lisa wheezed to a stop next to her.

"Yeah, but can you slow down a bit."

"Sorry," said Melina, who wasn't in the least bit out of breath. Her new bike seemed a lot easier to pedal than her old one.

After they'd cycled a couple of miles they pulled over, sitting down on a grass bank at the side of the road. Melina lay back with her head in her hands and stared upwards at the clear blue sky. All was quiet, with just a gentle hum from bees busy in the clumps of clover that were dotted amongst the grass. Lisa reached over into her saddlebag, took out the bottle of juice and took a long swig.

"I'm not sure I want to go all the way to Gatehampton Lock," said Lisa, before wiping her mouth, and passing the bottle to Melina.

"Oh go on, it's not far now, we're almost there. We turn off up here past the pig farm, and the path to Gatehampton is just past that."

After resting for a while, they continued on their way. A bit further on they came to a junction and turned off the main road down a narrow lane.

"I can smell the pigs, so it can't be far now," called Melina to Lisa, who was tagging along behind her.

They cycled past the pig farm, the curved metal pig houses glinting in the sun, and saw the pigs with their snouts down snuffling and snorting in the mud. A little further on they found a gate with a small signpost indicating the path to the woods and Gatehampton. After crossing a large grassy field, they entered the woods through a cut. A little way in they joined a wider, more open path that ran alongside a steep and wooded bank.

They hadn't been riding along for long when Melina pulled to a stop.

"What's that?" she said.

"What?"

"That white thing in the middle of the path. Over there."

As they got nearer they saw that what Melina had spotted was a large lump of chalk. It was so big it was blocking the path.

"It must have come from up there," said Melina, pointing through the trees to where a large section of the bank had fallen away, forming an enormous chalk pit. "Come on, let's go and take a look."

As they drew closer to the pit they could see piles of chalk all along the bottom. Amongst them were the twisted and shattered remains of trees that had once stood at the top. One huge lump still had topsoil and a large tree growing from it, its branches propping it up against the ground.

"There must have been a landslide," said Lisa.

"Let's see what it looks like from up there," said Melina.

After propping up their bikes against a tree, they climbed the bank at the side of the pit, and were soon standing at the top. Now much higher than the surrounding trees, they could see part of the field they had crossed below. Further off in the far distance was the main road with the red roofs of the Castle Field estate visible just off to one side.

They walked cautiously towards the edge and peered down into the pit. There was a solitary surviving tree growing out of the top edge. It was old and the bark along its trunk was split and peeling. It was tilted down and a gap had formed beneath the trunk, with some roots standing proud of the chalk. It had a few pale leaves on its one remaining small branch. A short length of frayed rope was tied around the trunk, dangling down into the pit.

"It's a shame that rope's so short, we could have had fun swinging on that," said Melina.

Then she spotted something. She crouched down to get a better look.

"I think I can see more rope under the tree. If you hold on to my legs, I'll see if I can reach it."

She got down onto her front, and then with Lisa kneeling across the backs of her legs, stretched out over the edge.

"I'm nearly there... that's it I've got it," she said, catching hold of the rope tentatively between her fingertips. "You can pull me back in now."

"There's miles of it," said Lisa, watching Melina coiling it up around her arm. "What are we going to do with it?"

"Tie it to the end of the tree of course."

"But we can't, it's too far out."

"One of us will have to climb out and tie it on," said Melina.

"I'm not climbing out there," said Lisa firmly.

"Oh well, I suppose I'll have to do it then," said Melina.

"No Melina, you can't, it's too dangerous."

"Aw, you worry too much. Here, hold onto this."

She handed one end of the rope to Lisa and then walked towards the tree, uncoiling the rope as she went. Dropping the remaining coils to the ground, she picked up the other end and looped it around her waist, finishing off with a knot.

"There, now as long as you hold on to that end I can't fall, can I?" said Melina, sitting down at the edge of the pit.

"Melina, please come back!" cried Lisa.

But Melina didn't hear her. She slid down until she was sitting astride the trunk, then, placing her hands in front of her, she started to shuffle along towards the far end.

She was about halfway along when the tree shuddered.

"It's moving!" shouted Lisa.

Melina stopped.

"What?"

"The tree, I saw it move. I don't think you should go any further."

"I didn't feel anything," said Melina and started shuffling forward again. When she got to the end she undid the rope from around her waist, then, leaning over and holding on with one hand, she passed the rope around the trunk.

"OK," shouted Melina, after making good with a large knot. "You can throw your end over the edge now."

Lisa threw it and it swung down below the tree, with the end settling just above the chalk face.

"There that should do it," shouted Melina.

She started to shuffle back along the trunk towards the edge. All of a sudden there was a loud crack. The chalk around the roots of the tree started to bulge, and then it lurched downwards. The tree was now tilting down at an alarming angle.

"MELINA!" shouted Lisa.

But it was too late. The ground around the base of the tree erupted as the roots surfaced and snapped. There was another loud crack, then the tree and Melina disappeared down into the pit. Seconds later, there was a thunderous crash and the ground shook.

"Melina!" shouted Lisa again. But there

was no reply. She walked over towards the edge and looked down. There was now a massive hole where the tree had been. Chalk dust hung in the air, and she could only just make out the bottom of the pit. The tree was lying at an angle with its roots pointing towards her. There was no sign of Melina.

"No, this can't be happening!" cried out Lisa, before collapsing in a heap on the ground. She sat there not knowing what to do. Then she heard Melina's voice.

"Lisa it's OK, I'm all right."

Lisa looked up. "Oh thank goodness!" she cried out. She could see Melina amongst the clouds of chalk dust, apparently floating in the air.

"Do you think you could find something to pull me back in?" said Melina.

"Hmm?"

"Can you find a long branch or something to pull me back in with?"

"Er – yeah. Hang on, I'll see what I can find."

"Hurry," said Melina.

There weren't any trees nearby, so Lisa had to go some way back before she found a branch that was long enough. She ran back and held out the end to Melina and pulled her back in.

They moved away from the edge and sat down side by side, looking out over the pit. A chalk dust haze was still hanging in the air, and they could barely see through it to the other side.

"You really had me worried there," said Lisa.

"I'm sorry, I wasn't thinking," said Melina, putting an arm around her.

"So how did you do it? I mean, why didn't you fall down there with the tree?"

"I did go down with it, but I managed to get away," said Melina. "I was in the air above it when it hit the ground."

"Oh, come on!"

"I know it's crazy. It took me a while to get used to it."

"So you just floated off it?"

"Yes. I seem to have gained this power that lets me float into the air."

"Do it again then," said Lisa, challenging her friend.

Melina stood up and moved a few feet away from Lisa. "OK, are you ready?"

"As ready as I'll ever be."

Melina's feet left the ground and she slowly floated up into the air.

"OK, you come down again now," said Lisa, when Melina was several feet up.

"So, do you believe me now?" said Melina, after she had landed safely back down on the ground again.

"Yes, I suppose so. So how long have you been able to do... well, that?"

"Oh, not that long, a month or so," said Melina.

"Why didn't you tell me?"

"I'm sorry. I was going to tell you yesterday in the cupboard, but I just couldn't do it."

"I thought that was strange," said Lisa. "I

bet it's fun being able to float like that."

"Yes, it's great," said Melina. "Although it's a shame I can't fly around. I can only go up and down. You must keep it a secret. I don't want anyone else to find out about it."

"OK," said Lisa, "nobody would believe me anyway."

Neither of them spoke for several minutes, each absorbed in their own thoughts. The sun disappeared behind a cloud and a breeze swept through the trees, stirring the leaves.

Lisa broke the silence.

"Melina, you know that fire? Do you think I could have started it?"

"What makes you think that?"

"I'm not sure, it's just that... well the fire seemed to spring up out of nowhere."

"Maybe you've got a power, like me. Let's see if we can make it happen again."

"What, you mean here? Now?"

"Yes."

"We might set fire to the woods," said Lisa.

"No, it'll be fine. We'll clear a patch of

ground and then there won't be anything to catch fire."

"But we haven't got a broom."

"Oh yes, I forgot about that. How about using that branch you just rescued me with?"

"Yeah, that might work," said Lisa.

They set to work clearing a patch of ground, and then Lisa went and stood in the middle.

"OK, when you're ready," said Melina from the side.

Lisa started waving the branch around frantically. "Fire, fire!" she shouted.

"Hang on, stop a minute," said Melina. "You weren't shouting fire when you were sweeping up, were you?"

"No," said Lisa.

"Well just do what you were doing," said Melina, a little impatiently.

"All right, all right," said Lisa. She began to move the branch again, more slowly this time, as if she were sweeping, but still nothing happened.

"Perhaps you were thinking about something special," said Melina. "When I want to float, I think about getting away from everything, and being very light."

"No, I wasn't thinking of anything," said Lisa.

"You must have been."

"No I WASN'T!" yelled Lisa, throwing down the branch in a rage.

Bright blue sparks leapt out from Lisa's fingers, crackling fiercely as they shot down into the ground. Pale blue smoke drifted up from the patches of earth where the sparks had struck.

"Wow!" said Melina, "that was amazing."

"But... but that's crazy, I shouldn't be able to do that."

"Well, at least we know how that fire started," said Melina.

"Yeah, I suppose we do. Perhaps..."

"Shush a minute," interrupted Melina, looking around and appearing puzzled.

"What is it?" whispered Lisa.

"I thought I heard something."

"It was probably the wind."

"No, it was a voice." She grabbed Lisa's arm. "There, did you hear it that time?" asked Melina nervously.

"No. I think we ought to go."

"Yeah, you're right. This place is starting to spook me out."

They made their way back down the side of the pit. As they reached the bottom, Lisa turned to Melina. "What was it you heard back there?"

"I heard a sort of muttering, and then someone said, 'She can hear us.'

"But how? There was no one there," said Lisa.

"I know, that's what freaked me out. I don't know about you, but I don't really fancy going any further. I'd rather set off back home."

"That's fine with me," said Lisa.

4

That afternoon the weather changed for the worse, and it started to spit with rain. Melina was lying on her bed, reading a magazine, but as she flicked through the pages the celebrities and stories inside were the last thing on her mind. The voice she had heard still troubled her. It had been a strange voice, high-pitched, and the owner had sounded annoyed at being overheard. But what bothered her most was that the voice had come from close by, from the direction of the pit, out of thin air.

Headlights sweeping across the ceiling

broke her train of thought. She crawled to the end of the bed and looked out of the window. A large black car had pulled up outside Lisa's house. Two figures wearing hooded coats got out of the car and walked up Lisa's drive. After a few minutes they reappeared. The rain intensified, hammering against the window, but she thought she could see someone else with them. They got into the car and drove off, leaving the road empty once more.

Melina awoke the next day to find that she had overslept. She got dressed and wandered downstairs. Her mother was in the kitchen.

"I wondered when you were going to surface," she said.

"I overslept," said Melina.

"Now, what are you having for breakfast? There's toast there."

Melina grabbed a slice of toast and spread it with a knob of butter. She went out of the back door, and then round to the side gate. As she walked up the short path to Lisa's front door she popped the last bit of toast in her mouth and pressed the doorbell. After a few moments Lisa's mother opened the door.

"Yes?"

"Hi. Is Lisa there?"

"Sorry?"

"Could I talk to Lisa?"

"Lisa?" enquired Mrs Wendell.

"Yes. Could I talk to her please?"

"We don't have anyone called Lisa here."

"What?" asked Melina, incredulously.

"I'm sorry, but we don't have a Lisa."

"But I'm Melina from... from next door."

"Yes, I know you are, said Mrs Wendell. And with that she closed the door.

There must be some misunderstanding, thought Melina. Maybe she didn't hear me properly. She pressed the doorbell again, and after a while Mrs Wendell answered it again.

"Could I see Lisa please?"

"I told you we don't have any Lisas here. Now, please don't bother me any more. Maybe you should try further down the road." And with that she closed the door again.

Melina's head was spinning. No Lisa? How could that be? She walked back down the path, her pace gathering with each step, tears welling up inside her. She crashed through the back door, slumped down at the kitchen table with her head in her arms, and then burst into tears.

"Good heavens, whatever's the matter?" asked her mother.

Melina didn't answer. She tried again.

"Melina, will you please tell me what's wrong."

"I just went next door to see Lisa," sobbed Melina, "and her mother said they didn't have anyone there called Lisa."

"Well, whatever made you think of doing such a strange thing? The Wendells don't have any children."

"No, that's not right, you know it isn't!" shouted Melina. "What's wrong with everybody?"

And with that, she got up from the table

and ran up the stairs to her bedroom. She flopped onto her bed, burying her face in her pillow. Her whole world had fallen to pieces; her best friend was gone, and worst still, forgotten.

Then she remembered the car and the strange hooded figures. Perhaps they had taken her, she thought. Yes, that's it; she'd thought she'd seen three figures coming away from the house last night; the third one must have been Lisa. But where had they taken her? And why didn't anyone remember her?

There was a knock on the door and her father called, "Melina, can I come in?"

"Hang on a minute." She sat up against the headboard and wiped her eyes.

"OK, you can come in now."

He came into the room smiling, peering down over the top of his bright red-rimmed glasses.

"I hear you're upset, something about a friend next door. Listen, why don't you come downstairs, you can help me with the car."

"I don't really feel like it at the moment," said Melina.

"Well all right, but don't stay up here too long." He bent over and kissed the top of her head, and then left her, closing the door behind him.

Her mind was still in a spin, going over the events of the last two days again and again. None of it made any sense. She got up and went downstairs. Joe was stretched out on the sofa watching TV in the living room. She sat down in the armchair opposite him.

"Joe?"

"Yeah?"

"You know Lisa?"

"Who?"

"Lisa, you know, from next door?"

"I don't know what you're on about."

"Lisa, my friend, Lisa?"

"Look, if you've got a new friend, what's it got to do with me?"

"She's not new, Joe, she's been round here loads of times. She was round here last week.

She broke your car, remember?"

"You're crazy, my car works fine."

"What?"

"It's over there if you don't believe me. See for yourself."

Melina walked over and picked up the car, then spun each of the chunky rubber wheels. But that couldn't be – Lisa had trodden on it. The front wheel had snapped off. Maybe Dad had fixed it?

"So it's been fixed then," said Melina.

"What?" asked Joe, not taking his eyes off the TV.

"The wheel on your car. Dad fixed it?"

"Yeah, if you like. Now can I watch this?"

****

That night it was still raining, and to make matters worse, a strong wind had blown up, making her window rattle. She lay there listening to the weather as it beat against the window, and eventually fell into a fitful sleep.

She was woken by the noise of the front doorbell. She sat up and drew back the curtains. The same black car she had seen the night before was outside the house. The bell rang again, and she heard voices in the hall downstairs.

Her mother called, "Melina, can you come down a minute?"

Melina froze.

"Melina dear, can you come down here please?"

Dear? thought Melina. *Mum never calls me dear.*

She opened the bedroom door and peered down over the banisters. Two hooded figures were standing in the hall, the two figures she had seen the night before last. She slowly made her way down the stairs.

"Ah, there you are, come over here, these nice people would like a word with you," said her mother, in a strange jovial manner.

The figures were a lot smaller close to, only four feet or so tall, and she could see now that the long black coats they were wearing were covered in fine silver netting. As she got to the bottom of the stairs the figure nearest her looked up and she saw inside its hood. It had no face, just two bright blue dots for eyes. The eyes began to change colour, first becoming pink, and then blood red. They became brighter still, and then began to flicker. Melina felt her strength ebbing away. Her legs gave way and she slumped to the floor. The last thing she remembered was her mother's face looking down at her, with that exaggerated and strangely fixed smile.

Upstairs in Melina's bedroom, strange things started to happen. The door swung shut and the curtains drew themselves. Things started to disappear: her school bag and books on the floor, clothes from various places around the room, her chest of drawers, her bed, the bookshelf with all her books and magazines, the toy cupboard, the mirrored wardrobe in the corner, her dressing gown on the back of the door and the pictures and posters on the walls. Finally, on the other side of the door, the small pink porcelain nameplate shaped like a bow with 'Melina's Room' stamped into it faded and vanished.

The same thing was happening in other parts of the house. In the bathroom her favourite soap disappeared, as did her other toiletries. In the living room, treasures of her past school projects vanished. Family photographs altered themselves, showing a proud family of just three, her mother, father and Joe. Her coats and shoes vanished from the hall cupboard. In the garage her bike faded out of existence, leaving just her brother's machine standing alone against the wall. Away from the house, anyone who had known Melina, knew her no more, as all memories of her were erased. Letters and documents altered themselves and the school register now showed one less pupil. It was as if Melina had never been born.

****

Surfacing as if from a deep sleep, Melina became aware of the noise of an engine. She was sitting in the back of a car, with one of the hooded figures just a few inches away from her. It was completely still now, looking straight ahead, its eyes extinguished, showing no sign of life. Looking out of the window, she recognised the houses and post box at the end of her road. Then there was a bright flash and the view disappeared, replaced by a fusion of swirling bright colours. The noise of the engine ceased, and the car felt like it was floating.

The inside of the car began to fade. Only small patches here and there at first, but gradually they merged into one another, causing whole sections of it to disappear. Even the seat she was sitting on was becoming invisible. After a while the car had completely disappeared. If she peered hard she could just make out the outline of the hooded figure next to her, sitting on the now totally invisible car seat. The swirling coloured light was now so close that she felt as if it was passing right through her. She closed her eyes to shut it out, but the colours were so bright she could still see them.

She had no way of knowing how long she had sat there, but after a while the intensity of the light reduced. She opened her eyes again. Things slowly started to appear, but she didn't recognize any of them. The seat she'd been sitting on was now a wooden bench, and the back of the seat in front was now just a simple wooden rail running across from one side to the other. The other figure was still sitting in front, its back against the rail in exactly the same position, completely motionless. But now, instead of holding a steering wheel in its strange purple hands, it was holding reins. The car had been transformed into a cart. Her eyes followed the reins to a large horse. The horse was still, and showed no sign of life. A tall building materialised nearby and the cart jolted, as if all four wheels had met the ground at the same time.

Where was this place? She wanted to run, to scream out, every one of her senses bristling, alert to any possible danger.

The figure next to her turned its head smoothly towards her, its eyes glowing blue once more.

"Ah, she… is… awake," it said in a deep voice. "No matter… we are… through now."

It rose slowly from the seat, got down, and came around to her side of the cart.

"Down," it grunted.

Melina sat still, not wanting to move away from the primitive safety of the cart. It was her only link with home, even if it had changed beyond all recognition from the car she had started out in.

"Down!" the figure grunted again, but more sternly this time.

She summoned all her courage and stood up, then gingerly stepped down from the cart.

It was good to feel solid ground under her feet again, even if it was in such a strange place. The horse snorted behind her, making her jump. She turned around. As far as she could tell it was the same horse, but now it was alive, shaking its head and pawing the ground, eager to be on the move.

"Come," said the figure, and then turned and walked away. The figure didn't touch her, but she could feel a strange pulling sensation, and felt compelled to follow.

They walked up a short flight of steps. At the top she looked back, but the horse and cart had vanished. She followed the figure beneath a large stone archway and entered a dimly-lit cobbled courtyard. She was very tired, her feet moving along sluggishly beneath her, and felt as if she was walking along in a dream. The figure led her to one side, towards another set of steps that climbed at a steep angle towards a studded wooden door. At the top of the steps he waved a hand and the door swung open to reveal a great hallway, lit by orange light.

Rising majestically off to one side was a wide stone staircase. At the top of each banister was the figure of a leaping lion, teeth bared.

She followed the figure inside, her footsteps echoing around the walls and disappearing into the expansive interior. She could hear only her own footsteps; the figure moved without making a sound. Passing the bottom of the stairs they went through another small door, and up a narrow spiral staircase. After passing through a door at the top, she found herself in a round room with long vertical windows. In the middle of the room was a low circular wall, about three feet high. The figure turned towards her, raised its arm and pointed to the wall.

"Climb," it grunted.

Melina turned to where it was pointing and saw that there was a narrow wooden platform on top of the wall with a small ladder leading up to it. She moved towards the ladder and began to climb it. On reaching the top she turned around, her fingers gripping tightly onto the posts on each side of the platform. At the other side of the wall was another much longer ladder. Her legs felt like jelly, and she felt sure she was going to fall, but somehow she managed to stay on.

She looked down. Below was another, smaller circular room, with two beds and a table with chairs. For a moment she thought the room was unoccupied, but then she noticed something that made her heart leap.

There was a sleeping figure in one of the beds. It was Lisa.

5

Melina stepped off the bottom rung of the ladder and ran over to the bed. "Lisa," she whispered, so as not to startle her, "Lisa, it's me, Melina."

Lisa raised herself sleepily onto one elbow and turned to look at her.

"Melina, is that really you? Oh, am I glad to see you!"

The two of them hugged. Then, sitting on Lisa's bed, Melina told her all the things that had happened since she had seen her last.

"But where are we, and why have we been

brought here?" asked Lisa.

"I'm not sure. From what I saw I'd say we're in a big house, or maybe even a castle. But I've no idea why we've been brought here. Have you seen anyone since you got here?"

"Well, sort of. Someone does come here. A boy, he brings food, but he always stays hidden up there, behind the wall. He sends the food down on a tray using ropes."

"Have you tried talking to him?"

"Yes. He doesn't say much. He told me not to be frightened because there are other young ones here."

"Young ones?" asked Melina, puzzled by the expression.

"Yes, I think he means children."

They heard footsteps above, and looked up.

"Food is coming," said a squeaky voice.

A tray descended from the wall above hanging between two ropes, just as Lisa had described, and landed gently on the ground. On the tray were two bowls of pea-green soup, bread rolls and mugs of milk. They took the food over to the small table and sat down. Melina picked up a bread roll and bit into it. Suddenly she realised that she was very hungry.

Melina finished the soup and bread off in double quick time. "Is this milk?" she asked, picking up the mug nearest her.

"I think so, but it's very creamy, you can't drink much of it."

The mugs were made of clay with a handle on each side, and they were heavy. Melina tried a little of the milk, holding the mug by both handles. It was warm and it did not taste as nice as the milk she had at home.

"Well, someone's got to come and see us sooner or later," said Melina. "Then maybe we'll find out why we've been brought here." She drank a little more of the milk, and then got up from the table and walked over to the other bed.

"If that's your bed, I guess this one's mine," said Melina. "I don't know about you but I'm exhausted."

She stretched out on the bed and rolled over onto her side, and was soon fast asleep.

Melina opened her eyes. It took her a few moments to work out where she was. She looked across at Lisa, who was still asleep, then she sat up against the headboard and surveyed the room. The walls had been constructed from huge curved stone blocks butted up against one another. There were no windows, but she could see what appeared to be daylight shining down over the wall above. She saw that the wooden ladder she'd climbed down was actually made in two parts, with the bottom half sliding up and over the top half. The bottom half had now been pulled up and was out of reach. There wasn't much furniture, just the two beds, two chairs and a table, which all seemed to be rather small.

Something caught her eye; a strip of dark polished wood, about three feet long, hanging vertically down the wall. She got up to examine it more closely. It had a brass metal plate running down the middle with two rows of weird-looking symbols. There was another much smaller silver plate with a hole in the centre sitting across it at one end. The plate had a wheel at each corner. One of the weird symbols was showing through the hole.

Lisa woke with a loud yawn. "Is it morning already?"

"I'm afraid so. Any idea what this is?"

"No, I hadn't noticed it," said Lisa.

A call came from above. "Food please."

The tray appeared, bringing them two bowls of steaming hot porridge and mugs of milk. After they'd eaten, they sat and waited.

"Perhaps we'll find out what all this is about today," said Lisa.

"I hope so," said Melina.

The voice called down to them again. "You have eaten?"

"Yes we're all done," shouted Lisa.

The bottom half of the ladder slid smoothly down until it was resting on the stone floor.

"Climb please," said the voice.

"Shall I go first?" said Melina.

"OK."

Melina got up from the table, walked over to the ladder and cautiously started to climb it. It wasn't until she was almost at the top that she saw the owner of the voice. She was so shocked that she nearly let go of the ladder. In front of her was a small man about four feet tall, dressed in a brown tunic, black breeches and leather ankle boots. He had a large head with small rounded ears at each side, which moved around like a cat's, and a bulbous nose. But the most surprising thing about him was that his skin was bright green.

"I am Merlot," he said, giving a wide grin which revealed sharp, pointy yellow teeth.

Melina stared, unable to believe what her eyes were showing her. Lisa, several rungs below her, noticed she had stopped moving.

"What is it?"

"It… it's a little man and he's green."

"What?" cried Lisa.

"The one with the squeaky voice. He's green."

"Oh come on."

"No, he is, honest."

The little green man took a couple of steps towards her, opening his hands in a welcoming gesture. "I am Merlot, and I am a Gamlyn. We will not hurt you."

His hands were big and chubby and they had only three fingers and a thumb.

"Well, we can't just stay here," called Lisa. "We'll have to trust him."

Melina moved up another rung, and then, still facing the same way so she could keep a wary eye on the strange little man, she descended the small ladder on the other side of the wall. Lisa arrived at the top and moved over next to her, grabbing hold of her hand and squeezing it tightly. "Follow me please," he said in a high-pitched voice.

He turned and walked to the door. Melina and Lisa looked at one another, unsure whether they wanted to follow, and neither wanting to make the first move.

The little man stopped and turned back

towards them. "Follow me please," he said again.

Melina moved slowly towards the door and Lisa followed, not wanting to be left on her own. They followed him down the stairs and across the hallway. The statues of the lions at the bottom of the main stairs looked less ferocious in daylight. For someone small he moved remarkably quickly, his stubby green legs whisking him along.

After passing through another door, they entered a long sunlit room, with tall arched windows. On the wall opposite was a long, colourful hanging depicting green men on horseback, some carrying swords, others long poles with pointed and hooked ends. At the end of the room, sitting in a high-backed chair behind an enormous wooden desk was another green man. This one had a long white beard. He was hunched over the desk looking through a pile of papers.

Merlot ushered them forwards. "Arrnult sir, I bring the two young ones," he said, with a small flourish of his hand.

"Ah, yes. Thank you Merlot," said the bearded man, in a surprisingly deep gravelly voice. He turned to the girls. "Please come a little closer," he said, smiling. "Now, what are your names?"

Neither of them spoke.

"Come now, no one is going to harm you."

Melina decided she had better say something. "Er... my name's Melina and this is Lisa."

"Welcome Melina and Lisa, please sit down," he said, gesturing to two chairs in front of the desk. "My name is Kurrok, and I am Arrnult of this castle. I hope you both slept well."

"Yes, yes we did thank you," said Melina.

"Well, I expect you're wondering why you have been brought here, and indeed, where here actually is. You will be surprised to learn that you are no longer in your own world. You have been transported across time and space to our world, a world of magic. This world is called Lia, which means 'mother' in Gamlyn, since it is from this world that we are born. Over the years we have managed to harness the magic of Lia to see into other worlds, such as your own. Whilst observing your world the Seers have seen young ones like yourselves doing strange things. Things that your kind would not normally be able to do."

"You mean like me be able to float into the air?" said Melina.

"Precisely."

"We discovered that the fabric of space between our worlds has been weakened, causing holes to appear. These holes are extremely small, but even so magic is leaking through them, from this world into yours. It is this magic that has caused you to develop these powers. For some reason we do not yet understand, it is only the younger of your kind who have been affected; the magic does not seem to have altered your elders.

"We decided that we could not just stand by and allow you to be changed in this way, so for some time now, we have been transporting young ones back here to have these powers removed. When we take someone from your world, we change things so that no one is aware that they are missing. Everything is then restored on their return, so it is as if they have never been away."

He paused to allow Melina and Lisa to take everything in.

"So, the voice I heard could have been one of the Seers?" said Melina.

"Voice?" said Kurrok, sounding agitated. "What voice was this?"

"I heard it a couple of days ago, we were in the woods," said Melina.

"And what did this voice say?" asked Kurrok.

"It said 'She can hear us.' It was odd, because there was no one there."

Kurrok rose from his chair, a stern look on his face.

"I am sorry, but I must ask you to leave now. I will call for Merlot and he will show you to the Focusing Room, where you can meet the others."

6

As Melina and Lisa rounded the corner, they could hear children's voices. The voices were coming from behind a small studded wooden door. Merlot opened it without knocking. A group of children were sitting behind small tables, laid out in the shape of a horseshoe, the gap pointing towards the front. Standing at the front was a large Gamlyn dressed in a yellow tunic and black breeches. He was no taller than Merlot, but he was bigger around the middle.

"Frydlic, I have the other young ones," said

Merlot.

"Ah, welcome, what are your names?" asked the big Gamlyn in a loud booming voice.

"This is Melina, and this is Lisa," said Merlot gesturing to each of them in turn.

"And what are your powers?" asked Frydlic, scowling at Merlot, since he had directed his last question at them and wanted them to answer.

"Well, said Melina, I have the power to float up into the air, and Lisa can make fire."

"Hmm, floating. Now that's one I have not come across before. And fire," he said, "very impressive." He turned to Merlot. "Thank you for bringing them to me." He ushered Merlot back out of the door and closed it behind him.

"Now, if you could both sit over there next to Shaun," he said, pointing to a dark-haired boy on the far side of the room towards the back, "I shall explain what we are going to do."

The room was long, with a high ceiling. It had a huge arched window at one end and smaller round windows high up along one side. There was a wooden table at the front, and sitting in the middle of it was a tall, highly-polished wooden box. Next to the box was a silver dome with a ruby red crystal held in a silvered clasp on top. The crystal caught the light from the windows, sending a red criss-cross pattern across the wall.

"If the others would just bear with me, I shall explain to Melina and Lisa what we are doing," said Frydlic. "Lenny here has the power of talking to others with his mind." He indicated a lean boy with springy ginger hair sitting at the front. "Over here on this table we have a pack of cards with a different symbol printed on each one. Before you arrived, Lenny had communicated the shape on one of these cards to me using his power to form that shape in my mind. He will now pick a different card and we shall do the same again, but this time he will be wearing the Focuser."

Lenny leant forward. Shielding the pack of cards from view, he picked out a card from the table. Frydlic picked up the silver dome and carefully placed it on Lenny's head. Once he was happy it was positioned correctly, he reached over to the wooden box on the table and slid open a door on the front. Inside the box was another much larger red crystal sitting in a silver cradle. The box started to hum. The humming grew louder, and then all of a sudden a beam of red light shot out towards the crystal on the Focuser, causing it to glow bright red.

Lenny concentrated hard on the card in front of him. A hush fell over the children as they watched. Frydlic stood absolutely still and closed his eyes. No one in the room made a sound, entranced by the scene in front of them. A few moments passed, and then Frydlic opened his eyes again. He leant forward and closed the box. The red beam was cut off and the crystal in the Focuser stopped glowing.

"That was excellent, Lenny," said Frydlic. "I could barely make out any shape at all that time. Thank you, you can return to your seat."

He looked across to where Melina and Lisa were sitting. "What you have just seen is the power of the Focuser to inhibit magical power. We shall do the same again tomorrow, and then again the next day, and each time it will reduce Lenny's power, eventually removing it altogether. Now Lisa, if you could join me."

Lisa got up, walked to the front and stood next to Frydlic.

"Now, Lisa, do you think you could you show us how you make fire?" Lisa looked at Frydlic with questioning eyes. "It's all right, just aim towards the stone floor just here," he said, moving her to a spot well away from the furniture.

"But I don't know how to make it happen," said Lisa.

"Oh,' said Frydlic, looking a little put out, since he hadn't had that problem before. "Can you tell me when it last happened?"

"Well, we were in the woods," said Lisa. "I'd been trying to make the fire happen without any success."

"I see. And when did it appear?"

"It was just after I'd shouted at Melina. I was annoyed with her, because she said I wasn't trying."

"Ah, I see. So it might be triggered by anger," said Frydlic.

"Yes," said Lisa, "that might be it."

"Well if you could think about that time again and how angry you were, we'll see if you can make it happen again."

"I'll try," said Lisa.

She stood there for several minutes, thinking about how angry Melina had made her, but nothing happened.

"Come on Lisa, you're not trying," Melina shouted from the back, realising that she had to get Lisa annoyed again, before she could make any fire.

"I am trying," protested Lisa.

"Well why isn't it working then?" continued Melina.

"I don't know," shouted back Lisa.

"Oh you're just being stupid, try harder," shouted Melina, winding her up more.

"What?" snapped Lisa.

Suddenly bright blue sparks flew out from her fingertips. Most of them hit the stone floor and fizzled away, but a stray spark hit the leg of Lenny's chair. The leg broke and the chair tipped sideways, sending Lenny sprawling across the floor. Lenny got up from the floor sheepishly and brushed himself down.

"Remind me not to get on the wrong side of her," he said grumpily. He found another chair further towards the back and sat down again.

"Ah", said Frydlic. "Your power is much stronger than I expected. I can see why you have been quartered away from others now." He picked up the pieces of the broken chair and put them in the corner. "Thank you Lisa, if you could return to your seat. Melina, perhaps I could ask you to come and show us your power."

Melina walked up and stood at the front next to Frydlic. He turned towards her and smiled.

"Now, don't force it, just do what you normally do."

Melina started to think about floating, and almost immediately her feet started to leave the ground. The other children gasped in amazement. Soon there was a large gap between the floor and the bottom of her feet. Slowly she drifted up towards the ceiling. She was about three feet off the ground when she heard a voice in her head. "Nice legs," it said.

Melina realised that it was Lenny who had put the words in her head. She looked straight at him and scowled. He sent her another message.

"Oops. Did I think that out loud?"

Melina turned her head away indignantly. When her head was level with the top of the door, Frydlic called her back down again.

"That was most impressive," said Frydlic, as she landed back gently on her feet. "A good example of controlling power, especially for one so young. Yes, very good. Now, I think it is time for a break." He turned towards a small girl with fair hair in the back row. "Mary, could you show Melina and Lisa where the food hall is please?"

"Yeah, no problem."

The food hall was just around the corner and down a short corridor from the Focusing Room. It was a long, dimly-lit room with huge oak beams and small square windows in the roof. There were wooden tables down each side of the room, with jugs of water and mugs on each one. Sitting down at a table near the door, Mary poured some water out into the mugs. There was a wide door halfway along the opposite wall, and the hubbub of frenzied shouting and clashing cooking utensils was coming from the other side.

"So have you just arrived?" asked Mary.

"Sort of, we've had one night here so far," said Melina.

"It's just that I haven't seen you in the dormitory."

"No we've been put somewhere else," said Lisa. "I think it's because they're worried about my power."

"Yes, that was pretty powerful stuff you did back there."

"Have you been here long?" asked Lisa.

"I think it must be about a week. My power's almost gone now," said Mary.

"What was your power?" asked Melina.

"Oh, I could tell what other people were thinking."

"Wow," said Lisa, "that must have been useful."

"No it wasn't, it was pretty awful. People don't want you to know what they're thinking. I tried to keep a straight face and think about other things to try and block them out, but it was always a struggle. Sometimes, if I wasn't concentrating hard enough I would reply to someone before they'd even opened their mouths, which annoyed them no end."

"So you're glad it's almost gone now?" asked Melina.

"Oh yes, it was a real nuisance," said Mary. The door opposite opened and a large

Gamlyn appeared carrying plates and a round wooden platter, with a large chunk of orange cheese and a small brown loaf sitting on top. He brought it over to their table.

"Enjoy," he said, in a way that suggested he was struggling to say it, and was not used to speaking English.

Mary cut off a piece of cheese and placed it on a plate. It was only then that she noticed that the other two weren't eating.

"Tuck in, I'm afraid you don't get much of a choice, the food's pretty basic here," said Mary.

Melina and Lisa started to eat. Melina liked the bread, but the cheese was much too strong for her taste, so she only had a small piece.

Once they'd eaten they returned to the Focusing Room.

"Right", said Frydlic looking down a list, "who's next? Ah yes, it's your turn Peter."

Peter, who appeared to be the oldest in the class and was definitely the tallest, got up from his chair and walked towards the front. As he passed Melina, she saw that he had bits of cotton wool sticking out of his ears.

"Peter has the power of exceptionally good hearing," said Frydlic, glancing down at his list again. He passed the Focuser to Peter. After removing the cotton wool from his ears, Peter placed it on his head. He had just finished putting it on when there was a knock on the door. After answering the door, Frydlic came back into the room looking somewhat perplexed.

"Melina and Lisa, would you come here please? The Arrnult wants to see you. Please go with this guard and he will take you to him."

The guard was dressed in a bright red tunic and black breeches with tall black boots, and he had a long sheathed sword at his side. He kept up quite a pace, and Melina and Lisa, who followed along closely behind, had a job keeping up with him.

7

Kurrok was sitting in front of a large stone fireplace, leaning forward and warming his hands in front of a roaring fire.

"Melina, Lisa, come in, come in, sit down," he said, beckoning towards two chairs at the other side of the fireplace. "I have called you back so I can finish what I wanted to say to you. If you remember, the last time we met I told you that you have been brought here to have your powers removed. Well, that is not the only reason."

He picked up a silver goblet from the small

round table next to his chair, took a sip from it, and replaced it.

"Perhaps I had better start at the beginning. Everyone has some kind of special power. Some might have a power that allows them to read minds, or move light objects. Others might have what you call second sight, where they can see things that others cannot. We are all born with those same weak powers. It has been like that for hundreds of years in this world. But it all changed after the discovery of the Sapphire Crystal. It is this crystal that gives us our magic, because when it is touched it enhances these powers, making them much, much stronger.

"Every few years, specially-selected young Gamlyns are taken to touch the Sapphire Crystal, to have their powers enhanced. They then join a select group called the Cullen, where they are taught how to control this power and use it wisely. A few years ago, a girl called Mydil was selected and taken to touch the crystal. The crystal made her more powerful than we had ever seen before, but it also made her twisted and evil. She has conjured up great fires, and many families have lost their lives. We have witnesses who have seen her standing and laughing at the sides of fires as they rage out of control, consuming all in their path. At other times she has been seen pointing a finger at some unfortunate person, and they have just melted away. One minute there, the next gone, never to be seen again.

"The latest sightings of her say that she has become old, her body bent and twisted. She is causing widespread panic, and some of the villagers have left their homes, preferring to live in the surrounding countryside rather than risk being trapped should she appear."

He reached over to his drink once more, his hand visibly shaking. He seemed to need it to steady himself before he could continue.

"Now, you remember I told you about the holes between our worlds. We have suspected for some time that Mydil was creating these holes, but we weren't sure until now. We think the voice you heard was her, and she is attempting to cross over from this world into your own. And, if you heard her, I am afraid to say, it appears that she has almost succeeded."

"What will happen if she gets through?" asked Melina.

"We cannot let her. It would destroy both our worlds. They are on different planes in time, and if the two should join, the sudden shift in time would tear our worlds apart."

Melina and Lisa looked at one another with horrified faces.

"But I don't understand. If it was Mydil I heard, who was she talking to?" asked Melina, breaking the silence.

"Talking to?" asked Kurrok.

"Yes, the voice I heard said *'she can hear us'*.

"Oh yes, I forgot to tell you. As well as making her very old, the magic from the crystal has driven her completely mad. She was probably talking to herself."

He fell silent again and stared into the fire.

"You said there was another reason why we've been brought here," said Melina, after a little while.

"Hmm?"

"You were going to tell us another reason for us being here."

"Yes... yes, so I was. Well, when we took Lisa from your world, we worked the same magic on you, as with all the other people who knew her, so that they would have no memory of her. But it had no effect, because you still realised that she was missing. This, we think, means that you have unusually strong powers. So we were hoping you would help us fight Mydil."

Melina gasped. "But I can't!" she cried. "How can I fight her? I can only float up in the air."

"No, you misunderstand me. You will not be sent as you are now. You will be taken to touch the Sapphire Crystal. Your power will be enhanced. You will become more powerful."

"But why does it have to be me?"

"Because Melina, you are special. Once you have touched the crystal, we believe that you will have something that no one else has – the power to fly. I do not expect an answer now. Sleep on it, and give me your answer in the morning."

He called for the guard and they were escorted back to their room. They sat down on the edge of Lisa's bed.

"Shouldn't we be going back to the Focusing Room?" asked Lisa.

"Well there's no point me going if I'm to stop Mydil," said Melina.

"You're going to do it then?"

"I don't know. I'm scared, she sounds very powerful, and I don't like the bit about her being mad."

The light was starting to fade, and Melina noticed that an orange globe had become illuminated in the roof. Merlot arrived.

"Food is coming," he cried down in a now familiar squeaky voice. A tray containing two steaming bowls appeared and moved down towards them.

"Careful, it is hot!" shouted Merlot.

They picked up the bowls and sat down at the table. Melina raised the bowl to her nose. "It smells good."

"What is it?" asked Lisa.

"I can't really see, it's too dark, but it smells like some sort of stew."

As they ate, Melina noticed that the room seemed to be growing brighter.

"Lisa?" she said.

"Mmm?" said Lisa, through a mouthful of stew.

"Is it me, or is it getting lighter in here?"

They looked up. The orange globe was floating just a few feet away above their heads.

"That's the globe from up in the roof," said Melina.

"So what's it doing down here?"

"Maybe they always come down at night. Or perhaps it heard me say it's dark and it came nearer to give us more light," joked Melina.

She got up from the table to inspect it more closely. Its surface was covered in small islands of a darker orange that moved around in ever-changing patterns. She was intrigued by it and reached out to touch it. In a flash, the globe moved up and stopped a few feet away, just out of reach.

"Did you see that?" asked Melina.

"Yeah, it moved really fast. Maybe you're not supposed to touch them."

Once they were in bed the globe dimmed, and then slowly drifted back up towards the roof.

8

Melina woke early the next morning. She couldn't sleep any more; her mind was just too busy. How could she defeat Mydil? She seemed so powerful – making fires – people disappearing? It was all so crazy.

Lisa woke and rolled over to face her, resting on one elbow. "Are you all right?"

"I didn't sleep very well," said Melina. "My head is still buzzing from what happened yesterday."

Merlot arrived with breakfast. They ate in silence, each absorbed in their own thoughts, and then waited for him to return.

"You have finished?" called Merlot.

"All done," said Melina.

The tray rose from the floor and disappeared up towards the roof. A few minutes later the ladder descended.

Melina was first to join Merlot at the top. She moved over to look out of one of the windows. They were equally spaced around the curved walls and set back inside the thick walls of the castle. The panes of glass were crudely made with a rippled surface that distorted her view. She could just make out a large lawn with a path down one side.

She moved around to another window. The view was now of small walled gardens, filled with brightly coloured borders. She thought she could see a mountain in the distance.

Lisa arrived at the top of the ladder and came over to join her. "It looks lovely."

"Yeah," said Melina, sounding somewhat deflated, because she wanted to be outside.

Merlot wandered over to join them. "We

have to go now, we must not keep the Arrnult waiting," he said.

As they walked down the stairs, Melina asked Merlot about the globes of light.

"Ah, you mean the orbs," said Merlot. "We have not had them long, they were a gift from the Cullen."

They arrived at the Arrnult's room. His door was open and he was at his desk, writing with a large quill pen. He looked up as they approached.

"Ah, come in. Now Melina, have you got an answer for me?"

"Yes," said Melina. "I'll help you. I'll help you defeat Mydil."

"Excellent!" said Kurrok, looking relieved. "There is one other thing that I should mention though, and that is that what we are about to do must be kept secret. If the Cullen were to find out that you have been to visit the Sapphire Crystal, there would be an outcry. Now, if you stay here, I shall make the arrangements."

"Kurrok sir," called Melina as he was almost at the door.

"Yes?" said Kurrok, turning around.

"Do you think it would it be possible for Lisa to come to the crystal with me?"

"Ah, that would not be wise," he said, shaking his large green head, which made the end of his long white beard do a little dance.

"Please, it would make it so much easier for me," pleaded Melina.

Kurrok stroked his beard thoughtfully. "Well I suppose I could allow it, since you will have to be blindfolded anyway. Yes, Lisa may accompany you."

Kurrok seemed to be gone for ages, but when he did finally return a small older-looking Gamlyn in a brown woollen cloak and two guards accompanied him.

"This is Huron," said Kurrok. "He is our oldest Seer, and was once the leader of the Cullen, so he knows the ways of the Sapphire Crystal. Merlot will now put blindfolds on you. Please say if they are too tight."

Once Merlot was sure they couldn't see anything, he beckoned to the guards and they walked slowly towards the door, with Merlot holding Melina's arm to guide her and one of the guards guiding Lisa.

"Is it very far?" asked Melina.

"I cannot tell you. But do not worry, we are not walking all the way, we will be going most of the way by cart."

She felt a slight breeze on her face as they walked outside. "Careful," said Merlot, pulling gently on her arm, "there are steps to go down here."

Melina felt for the edge of each step with her foot and stepped down carefully. They got to the bottom and started walking more normally again. Then, after another smaller set of steps, they were at the cart. Merlot guided her to her seat. Lisa joined her a few moments later. The driver called out in some strange tongue and the cart moved off with a jolt.

Melina could feel the warmth of the sun on her back. "I wish we could see, it feels like such a lovely day," she said.

How much further they travelled before Merlot spoke again, they had no way of knowing.

"We are here," he said.

The cart rocked as he jumped down from it. Minutes later it moved forward again and then stopped suddenly, as if it had hit something. In that moment Melina felt as if she'd been transported to another place, and a door had been closed, sealing her in. The air smelt musty, and it was cooler. A little way off she could hear the sound of dripping water.

"You can take your blindfolds off now," said Merlot, his voice echoing strangely.

Melina removed her blindfold and rubbed her eyes. It seemed impossible, but they had left the bright sunshine and trees behind and were now inside a cave. The floor was not level but sloped upwards towards one wall. There was a small tunnel in the wall, and the light from it was lighting the cave.

"It's on foot now," said Merlot, as they got

down from the cart. "Just through there," he said, pointing to the tunnel. "But please keep your heads down. The ceiling is low."

They followed Merlot and Huron into the tunnel, the guards behind them. The floor of the tunnel seemed to be sloping downwards. Melina became aware of a blue light, which appeared to be getting brighter with each step.

As they came out of the tunnel they found themselves in another, much larger, cave. The walls were a mixture of a dark black slate-like rock and blue crystals formed in layers. The mysterious blue light was coming from the narrow crystal layers. There were several huge rock columns in the middle of the cave which disappeared up into the darkness towards the roof, its existence only given away by huge folds of slate-black rock, hanging down like the ragged wings of giant bats.

"It's beautiful," said Melina, running her hands carefully along the edge of one of the crystal layers.

"This way," called out Merlot, "but be

careful, the floor is slippery."

They followed the direction of his voice, trying to avoid treading on the blue crystals that spread out in a patchwork across the cave floor.

"Woah!" cried out Lisa suddenly, losing her balance and grasping hold of Melina's shoulder to stop herself from falling.

"Are you OK?" asked Melina, after her friend had found her feet again.

"Yes, thanks. I can't say the same for those though," she said pointing to a small pile of crystals which she'd dislodged from the cave floor.

"Don't say anything, I don't think anyone noticed," whispered Melina.

They moved on, being more careful where they were placing their feet in case they dislodged more crystals. As they got closer they could see Merlot and Huron standing next to a large pool of water. Towering upwards in the centre of the pool was an enormous sapphire-blue crystal. It was shaped like an egg, and the sides were covered in jagged ridges that spiralled around from top to bottom. The top of the crystal was at eye level, and it was so big around the middle it would have been impossible for anyone to reach around it and touch hands at the other side. The light inside it was more intense than the surrounding crystals, and it shimmered and spun around in an ever-changing display, reflecting off the surface of the water in little patches which seemed to play a game of chase on the walls.

"Melina, if you could come over here please?" said Huron, breaking her out of her trance. "And Lisa, if you would stand over there by the wall with the guards."

"Good Luck," said Lisa.

Melina edged nearer to the crystal.

"If you would stand there," said Huron, pointing to the floor, where a complete circle of blue crystals had formed. Melina stepped carefully into the circle.

"In a moment," said Huron, calmly in a low

voice, "I'm going to ask you to reach a hand out slowly towards the Sapphire Crystal. As you get nearer you may see rays of red light leaping towards your fingers. If you do, hold your hand still until they disappear. The most important thing to remember is that once you are touching the crystal, you must not let go until I say."

He took out a small round red crystal with a tiny well in the top and placed it on a ledge above the Sapphire Crystal. As Melina watched, a drop of water dripped down from the ledge above and fell into the well. After several more drops the water was visible at the top. Another drop fell and the well overflowed, dripping down onto the Sapphire Crystal below.

And then it happened. It was as if the Sapphire Crystal had awoken. The light from it intensified, flooding the cave with a dazzling bright blue light.

"All right," said Huron. "If you could start moving your hand out towards the crystal?

That's it, not too fast."

Melina tried hard to keep her hand from trembling as she reached out. She couldn't think how she was supposed to see the rays of red light that Huron had mentioned amid the intense light of the crystal. But then, they were there, accompanied by a strange tingling sensation in her fingertips. She kept her hand still. The tingling subsided and the lines disappeared, just as Huron had told her. She moved her hand forward again, wondering how much further it would be before her fingers touched the crystal. The red rays appeared once more. Her arm was getting tired. The rays disappeared, and she edged forward again.

Her fingers touched the crystal, and an electric shock shot up her arm. She was jerked backwards up into the air. In the blink of an eye she was far above the crystal. She felt a sharp pain in her back as it met with the jagged roof of the cave. Then she started to fall back down, the crystal circling crazily beneath her. She landed in a crumpled heap in a pool of icy water. The crystal was now towering above her.

She got back on to her feet and walked around it, wading through the knee-deep water. Squinting, she could just discern a round doorway above the waterline. Stepping through it, she found herself in a circular room. A spiral staircase jutted out from the crystal wall, as if the wall itself had been pushed inwards to create it. She started to climb it. Each step looked identical to the next. After a while she began to wonder if she was maybe just treading the same steps over and over again, and not actually going anywhere at all.

But then she arrived at the top.

Stretching out in front of her was a long, thin hall with massive crystal pillars down each side. Everything in the hall was made of crystal, but it was giving out very little light, except for a small patch on the rear wall which was glowing brightly. She walked towards it, careful not to trip on the uneven floor. The patch was about three feet wide and was glowing bright blue, lighting up the crystal floor in front. As she approached it, a crack appeared and travelled down the wall. More cracks appeared, and part of the wall fell to the floor, smashing into tiny pieces. Each piece tinkled as it hit the floor again and again before finally coming to rest. A small recess had formed in the wall.

Melina walked a little nearer, her trainers crunching on the broken crystal. Inside the recess was the whole of the Sapphire Crystal Cave in miniature, the scene lit by the light from the crystal. Everything in the recess was perfect in every detail. She could see herself, with her hand held out towards the Sapphire Crystal and Huron and Merlot close by. She could even see them moving, their faces looking anxiously towards her.

But something didn't seem quite right. There was a small green face to one side of the crystal, and it was getting bigger. In an instant it flew out from the recess and straight through her. She felt a sharp stabbing pain and then felt very cold, as if a large block of ice had formed inside her stomach. She tried to run, but her legs refused to obey her.

The face moved away, and then came back towards her. It was now several feet across. It was the gnarled and deeply wrinkled face of an old Gamlyn woman, her sunken bloodshot eyes and blackened lips curled back in a maniacal grin, showing several rotten orange teeth. She had a mass of wiry white hair. "You're going to die!" it cackled.

The warmth returned to Melina's body and she ran, stumbling down the stairs to get away. The cackling was following her, getting closer, louder. She desperately wanted to turn her head to see how near it was, but she was afraid that if she did she might lose her footing and fall. Reaching the bottom of the stairs she ran straight out through the doorway, and then stopped abruptly.

"No!" she screamed. "It can't be!" She was

back in the hall, and the wizened old face was coming towards her once more. But it had now grown even bigger, and stretched from floor to ceiling. The eyes were staring straight at her, filled with hatred. The enormous mouth opened. "You're going to die... die... die!" it said, spitting the words out with venom.

It rushed towards her and she fell backwards, realising too late that she was at the edge of the stairs. She tumbled down, her body colliding painfully with each step as she fell. Through the pain she could hear someone calling her name.

"Melina, let go, let go!"

It was Huron. She remembered that her fingers were still touching the crystal.

I... must... move... my hand, she thought, desperately trying to drag herself back to consciousness. *I've... got to... let go.*

She became aware of someone shaking her shoulder. Huron was crouching over her.

"I thought we'd lost you," he said.

"Mydil!" she gasped.

"It's all right Melina," said Huron. "You're safe now."

"But her face kept growing," said Melina. "It went through me, and I was so cold."

"I'm sorry. It seems she has found a way inside the crystal. She must have realised that you are a threat to her, and she was trying to make you let go before the crystal could work its magic."

"Did she succeed?" asked Melina.

"We can only hope that she did not," said Huron. "Now, let's get you back to the castle."

On the way back Melina was very tired and fell asleep on Lisa's shoulder. Lisa shook her gently to wake her as they arrived back at the castle.

"Are we here?" asked Melina.

"Yes," said Merlot, "you can take your blindfolds off now. The Arrnult said he wanted to see us the moment we returned."

They removed their blindfolds, got down from the cart and walked back towards the main entrance.

"Right," said Kurrok, once they were seated. "Tell me exactly what happened, and please don't leave anything out. Even the smallest detail could be of use to us."

Melina told him what had happened after she had touched the crystal.

"I see," he said when she'd finished. "It looks as if she has found her way inside the crystal. This is bad, very bad."

He got up and paced around the room. Melina's eyes followed him. She was thinking that all this seemed so familiar now, and that despite his small stature and unusual appearance, she was listening to him as though he was now her leader as well.

"Well," he said, "I don't see that there is any more we can do today. I think you should rest now. Tomorrow we shall see if we can discover what effect the Sapphire Crystal has had on you."

9

When they joined Merlot at the top of the ladder the next day, there was a guard with him.

"Lisa, this guard will take you to the Focusing Room," said Merlot. "Melina, please come with me."

"Where are we going?" asked Melina as she followed Merlot past the bottom of the stairs and down a narrow corridor to one side.

"To see Huron. He is skilled in the art of sensing, and so will be able to tell if the crystal has changed you."

A little way along the corridor, they arrived at a small wooden door. Merlot rapped on it with the back of his hand. There was muttering from the other side, and then it creaked open.

"Ah, come in," said Huron. "I have been expecting you."

The room was tall, with an arched brick roof. Bookcases, crammed to bursting, covered every wall, with many of the books only lodged in part way. Piles of books were scattered about the room, some waist high, each book haphazardly stacked upon another, looking like it was only a matter of time before they toppled over. The room was bright and sunlight was streaming in from a large window, which looked out over a garden. A wooden desk stood in front of the window with a large stone chalice, or cup, on top.

"If you would sit there, please Melina," said Huron, gesturing towards a chair just in front of the desk.

Melina carefully navigated her way around

the piles of books and sat down. Huron pulled up another chair, and sat opposite.

"I've been asked to carry out a sensing in order to tell if the Sapphire Crystal has worked its magic. It is a simple process and quite painless, so please just try to relax."

He picked up a small glass bottle, pulled out the cork and turned it upside down over the chalice. Something fell inside, making a tiny splash.

"A small piece of blue crystal, in case you are wondering," said Huron. "Now, please come a little closer, I promise not to bite," he added with a grin. Melina could see that he had lost all his teeth, apart from one in the middle of his bottom jaw which jutted out at an alarming angle. She shuffled her chair a little nearer, scraping it noisily across the stone floor.

"Good," said Huron. "If you would place your right hand on the handle of the chalice. That's it, not too tight. Now, I need you to completely empty your mind. If you find you have trouble with this, imagine you're looking into the chalice and it's completely empty."

'I'll try,' said Melina, a little nervously.

Leaning forward, Huron grasped the other handle, then closed his eyes. He began to mutter, reciting the same word over and over again and swaying gently from side to side.

"Armanom... armanom..."

Blue smoke appeared, and began to swirl around inside the chalice. The smoke thickened until the bottom of the chalice was completely obscured. The handle began to vibrate.

"Ah" said Huron. "Yes, yes. I see you now. You are flying high in the sky. I see the ground rushing past beneath you at great speed. But there is a look of concern on your face. Something is up ahead. A forest. I see tall trees. Good... good, you are climbing higher to avoid them. But the vision... is fading."

The swirling blue smoke in the chalice slowed. Huron's brow wrinkled as he concentrated. He began to mutter again.

"*Armanom... armanom...*"

The smoke began to swirl once more. Melina tried to concentrate, clearing her mind. A moment passed and then Huron spoke again.

"I see. Yes, yes. You are flying again, but much nearer to the ground this time. I see someone else there, but I cannot see who it is. I see a bright flash, and someone else has appeared – no, some*thing* else. Something is near you, something big. But, no it is fading again – it has gone."

The swirling gradually slowed until the blue smoke was barely moving. Huron stopped swaying. After a short time he rejoined them, coming back out of his trance. He opened his eyes slowly and blinked several times, stretching his eyes wide. After a time he spoke.

"What I saw was very impressive. You were flying at great speed and appeared to be able to change direction with ease. I saw also that you might have a second power, just as we had hoped. But the images were fading so fast I'm afraid I was unable to discern this power. We could try again, but I fear I would not see more.

"But we must not be disheartened. I was concerned at the cave that you might not have been touching the crystal for long enough. Well, I am glad to say that it seems I was worrying unnecessarily. The visit to the crystal has been a total success. The crystal has done all we had hoped for, and perhaps more."

"That's great news," said Melina, "but when will I actually be able to fly?"

Huron smiled. "All in good time my dear. We have not had anyone who could fly before. We will have to work out a way we can observe you flying whilst you learn its art; after all, you have the power, but do not know how to use it yet. We will need to find somewhere with enough space, but where nobody can see you."

He stood up and stretched his back, and

then walked over to talk to Merlot. After a few minutes he returned, smiling.

"The final decision will have to be made by Kurrok of course, but we think we might know a place where you can learn to fly."

"Excellent news," said Kurrok, after Huron had described what he had seen at the sensing. They were sitting in Kurrok's office once more.

"Now, how are we going to train you, Melina? It will have to be done in secret."

"We were thinking of using the Great Tower," said Huron.

Kurrok stroked his beard thoughtfully.

"Hmm, do you think there is enough room inside? We cannot risk her going too high and being seen."

"We think so. We thought we could tie a rope around her, so that she cannot rise above the tower walls," said Huron.

Melina pulled a face. "Do I really need a rope around me?"

"Yes, I'm afraid it will be necessary," said Huron. "If you fly too high someone might see you. And we need to keep your power a secret."

"The Great Tower it is then. Could you make the arrangements Merlot? I think you should start straight away, Melina. There is no time to lose." They got up from their chairs and started towards the door. "Oh, and one more thing. Mydil and the Cullen must not find out about this, so please make sure that Melina is not seen when you take her to the tower."

"Yes, of course," said Merlot.

Merlot took Melina along to the food hall, telling her he had to go and make arrangements at the tower, but would be back to collect her later. She hadn't been sitting long when she heard children's voices, and the other children joined her, Lisa amongst them.

"Hi, I didn't expect to see you in here today," said Lisa, sitting down next to her. Keeping her voice low, Melina told Lisa what had happened at the sensing.

"So you will be able to fly?" whispered Lisa. "That's amazing."

"Yes, and Huron thinks I might also have another power, but he couldn't see the vision clearly enough to tell what it was."

Melina glanced across to the table on the other side of the hall. Lenny was sitting on the end of the bench facing her. He saw her looking and smiled back.

A wooden platter carrying a small brown loaf and two bowls of broth arrived at the table.

"And this Great Tower is where they're going to teach you to fly?" asked Lisa, tearing off a piece of bread.

"It sounds like it," said Melina.

"I wish I could come with you."

"I don't think you can this time. Sorry."

"Anyway tell me what you've been up to," said Melina. "Have you had a go with the Focuser yet?"

"Yes, just now, said Lisa. "It was a bit weird

putting it on, and when Frydlic opened the box on the table and the red beam hit it, I felt this sort of tingly feeling where it was touching."

"Do you feel any different?"

"Well no, not really. And I couldn't see any change in the fire from my fingers either. I suppose I wouldn't after just one go. But Frydlic seemed very pleased."

"Did anyone else have a go?"

"Er… Mary. Oh yeah, and Peter had another go, you know the boy with the sensitive ears," she said, giggling. "I shouldn't laugh really, but it was so funny. It was all going fine. He'd taken the cotton wool out of his ears, and put the Focuser on, and then Frydlic had whispered something to him. But as he was taking the Focuser off, Lenny let out a huge sneeze. Peter nearly shot through the roof. They had to take him away to see the nurse."

Merlot returned and walked over purposefully to their table.

"Well, you seem to be enjoying yourselves."

"Lisa was just telling me what happened at the Focuser this morning," said Melina.

"Good, good," said Merlot, appearing somewhat preoccupied. "I came to say that we are ready for you."

Melina got up from her chair.

"Good luck," said Lisa.

"Thanks, I've got a feeling I might need it," said Melina.

10

Melina followed Merlot out through the main door and down into the courtyard. After crossing the courtyard, they entered a gloomy-looking tunnel. At the end Merlot pushed on a small wooden door, and it swung open to reveal a large lawn. The sky was blue with only the odd little white cloud scattered here and there, not one of them grown up enough to be full-blown rain clouds.

Crossing over the corner of the lawn, they followed a gravelled path and came upon an ivy-covered stone wall. There was an archway halfway along the wall surrounded by little pink flowers, and after walking through it Melina found herself in a large walled garden. A myriad of different plants lined the walls, some of which she recognised, or at least thought she did, since some of the shapes looked vaguely familiar. The edge of each colour-filled border was edged with small white stone pyramids.

The scent from the flowers was heavy and sweet, and helped take her mind off what she was about to do. It would have been lovely just to lie down there next to the stones. Perhaps if she closed her eyes, she thought, when she opened them, she would find herself back home, in her own garden, with everything back to normal. But she knew it wasn't that easy. Mydil had to be stopped or she would destroy everything.

There was a small door at the far corner of the garden, and after walking through to a more open patch of ground, she saw the tower off to one side.

"The Great Tower is part of the original, much older castle," said Merlot, as they approached it. "They used most of the stones from the old castle to build the new one, but left the old tower intact."

Melina followed Merlot around the base of the tower, the huge curved walls looming over them. There was a Gamlyn-sized opening in the wall, and she had to duck down to avoid hitting her head as she went through.

The ground inside the tower was grass-covered, apart from a small stone path that led from the opening to a partly-demolished spiral staircase at the other side. The roof was missing, and the top of some of the wall had crumbled away. Huron was standing next to a large wooden table over to one side, next to the tower wall.

"Hello Melina, how are you feeling?" he asked.

"Um, a little nervous."

"Well try not to be, I'm sure you are going to do just fine. You can take your cloak off now. No one can see you inside these walls."

Melina removed her cloak and tucked it under the table.

"In a moment I'll ask you to use your power to float into the air. Once you're in the air, we can begin the next stage, which will be to work out what it is you need to do to fly from one place to another. But first we will need to put a tether on you to stop you flying up too high."

He turned towards Merlot.

"Merlot, over on the table you'll find some rope and a metal spike. Could you bang the spike in somewhere near the middle, and tie the rope to it?"

Once he'd finished banging the spike in, Merlot returned holding the other end of the rope.

"What do I do with this?"

"Ah yes, we need to tie that end around Melina's waist to stop her going up too high. After all, we don't want to lose our star pupil do we?" he said, with a little chuckle.

Merlot tied the end around Melina,

checking the knot carefully to make sure that it wouldn't slip.

"Right, if you are ready Melina," said Huron. "Please go and stand next to the spike over there."

Melina walked over and stood in the middle of the grass with the spike just to the side of her.

"In your own time then," said Huron.

Melina started to think about floating. Then suddenly – *WHOOSH!*

The speed at which she left the ground startled them all. Merlot had to jump sideways as the rope flew up into the air next to him. Next the spike, which should have stopped her from going up too far, shot up out of the ground, scattering lumps of turf everywhere. Melina, rope and spike disappeared up into the sky. In the blink of an eye she was high above the clouds. As she came to her senses, she felt very cold. *I must not go any higher,* she thought. *It will get colder higher up.* Her speed slowed a little.

She thought about how lovely it would be to be back down on the ground, and her speed slowed a bit more. After one more go, she was relieved to find she was going back down.

Through the clouds she could see the tower, a small, just distinguishable circle directly below. She felt a cold dampness on her skin and shivered as she passed into a cloud. Minutes passed by as she drifted through it, unable to see anything but the odd glimpse of blue sky. She eventually came out below the cloud. Looking down past her feet she was relieved to see the familiar scene of the colourful walled gardens. The tower was directly below her.

As she dropped lower, something caught her eye. A huge black bird was sitting on top of the tower wall, looking up at her. Merlot was shouting out to her, and waving his arms.

"Melina, you are going to hit the wall. Move away!"

She thought about moving sideways, but nothing happened. She lost more height.

"That way!" she shouted anxiously, raising one hand. Almost immediately she flew off and then over the lower part of the wall, missing it by inches. The ground flashed past by below her at an alarming speed. There were tall trees in front of her. She thought about moving upwards to avoid them, lifting her arms a little as she did so, and gained height. Skimming over the treetops, she looked down into the green canopy below.

She discovered that if she held both hands out in front, all she had to do was twist and point in the direction she wished to go. Now she had control she started to relax and began to enjoy herself. She turned around and headed back towards the tower.

As the tower came back into view, she noticed that the bird she had seen earlier had disappeared. She saw Merlot and Huron waving to her below as she circled the tower, gradually reducing her speed. As she got lower, she brought her arms back down to her side. She landed with a jolt, bending her knees, and rolled over onto her side.

Merlot rushed up to her, his face beaming. "I thought we had lost you," he said.

"Well done Melina, that was most impressive," said Huron, joining them.

"I couldn't control where I was going to start with, but after I stopped panicking, I got the hang of it," said Melina.

"Well that wasn't quite what I had in mind, but you certainly seemed to have worked out how to fly," said Huron.

Suddenly there was a loud screech. Melina saw a fast-moving shadow sweeping across the grass towards them.

"Get down!" she cried, throwing herself at Merlot and Huron, pushing them to the ground. A large bird flew over them with its talons extended.

"Quickly!" shouted Melina, "get under the table before it comes back."

They helped Huron back to his feet and ran towards the table. There was plenty of room for all three of them underneath, although Melina's head was touching the underside.

She hadn't noticed before, but now saw that she still had the rope around her waist. It was trailing out over the grass, so she pulled it back in and coiled it up next to her.

The bird landed a few feet away. All of a sudden it ran towards them, screeching loudly and flapping its wings menacingly, its long curved orange beak wide-open.

Melina lashed out with her foot. "Get away, you horrid bird!" she shouted.

The bird screeched and hopped backwards, then sat looking at them from a short distance away.

"Well done Melina, but we need to get away from here," said Merlot. "I think it will attack again. See that gap in the wall over there? When I say, make a run for it, and I'll stop it attacking you."

"But you'll be hurt," said Melina.

"No, you must go."

Merlot reached up over the top of the table and brought down the mallet.

"Wait for my signal."

He crawled out from under the table and stood up slowly, keeping a wary eye on the bird. Then he ran straight for it, waving the mallet above his head and shouting menacingly, "RAH! RAH!"

The bird leapt up and took to the air. It circled overhead squawking loudly.

"Now," shouted Merlot, "go quickly."

Melina grabbed the coil of rope and crawled out from under the table. She offered a hand to Huron and pulled him to his feet, and then they ran towards a narrow gap in the wall. But the bird spotted them, and flew back down. Merlot moved swiftly, putting himself in between them and the bird, and they ran behind him. They arrived at the gap and climbed through. Melina stopped as she got to the other side and turned to Huron.

"We can't leave him on his own against that thing."

"We have to," said Huron.

"No," said Melina, "you go on, I'll go back and help him."

She climbed back through. Peering around the edge of the wall she could see Merlot was only a few feet away from the bird. He moved closer. Suddenly holding the mallet out in front of him, he made a dive at it. But he missed, the mallet thudding into the ground several inches away from it. The bird was alarmed, but unharmed and hopped away a short distance. Merlot, however, was lying on his front next to the path, not moving.

Melina realised that something was wrong. She moved out from the safety of the gap, trying to think of some way she could save him. Uncoiling a few turns of the rope, she let the spike drop down onto the grass and moved into a position between Merlot and the bird. She didn't have long to wait before it attacked again. She whirled her arm around, sending the rope and spike forwards. The bird gave a startled screech and flew back as the spike came down to one side with a loud thud. Melina pulled on the rope again, drawing the spike towards her.

"Come on then!" shouted Melina, trying to sound brave, although she wasn't feeling it.

As if it understood the challenge, it flew back up into the air. It circled overhead screeching, and then swooped down again. Melina kept her eye on it, standing to face it as it flew towards her. It was almost within striking distance of the spike. Just a bit closer, she thought. Then all of a sudden, it changed direction and flew around the other side of her, away from the spike. Its sharp talons tore into her shoulder and held tight. She dropped the rope and tried to beat it off with her other hand, but couldn't reach far enough over to make it let go. Panic stricken, she ran back towards the table, but as she ran she was tripped by the rope and fell. The bird released its grip as she hit the ground and flew away, landing just a few feet to the side of her.

Melina lay completely still. The bird cocked its head from side to side, watching. It gave a long victorious screech and hopped back towards her. Quick as a flash she turned over, swinging the spike in an arc. This time it connected, hitting the bird squarely across the beak. It staggered back, shaking its head. She quickly got back on to her feet, and ran towards it shouting, "RAH!"

The bird jumped back away from her, jumped again and then flew drunkenly into the air, narrowly missing the tower wall. Melina watched it fly away, and then hurried over to Merlot. She crouched over him and gently shook him by the shoulder.

"Merlot, Merlot wake up."

Merlot opened his yes. "Ow, my head!" he groaned. He rolled over onto his side and sat up slowly. There was a large bruise on his forehead where he had hit the stone path.

"You've got quite a bruise there," said Melina.

"You are injured too," he said looking at the blood on her shoulder.

Huron climbed back through the gap and came towards them. "Has that thing gone?" he asked.

"Yes," said Melina, "for now."

"I think we ought to get you both back to the castle and let the nurse have a look at those injuries," said Huron.

"What sort of bird was that?" asked Merlot, as they walked back to the castle.

"A Mantle Eagle," said Huron, "I've seen them around here before, but I've never heard of anyone being attacked by one."

"I saw it sitting on the tower wall earlier," said Melina, "when I flew back here. It seemed to be watching me. Do you think Mydil sent it?"

"It is possible," said Huron, "they do say she used to have a way with animals."

Once back inside the castle, they went straight to see the nurse. Melina's shoulder was starting to hurt, and she was very relieved when they finally arrived. The door was open and they walked inside. The room was small, and apart from the desk and a set of small shelves on the wall holding a few coloured bottles, it was fairly bare. Merlot sat her down on a chair.

It wasn't long before the nurse arrived. She spotted Merlot first, leaning against the wall.

"Merlot, what do you want?" she said in a voice that could have cut through concrete. "If it's more pills for one of those headaches of yours, you can forget it, we haven't got enough to keep giving them out to you every time you have too much to drink."

She was short and very plump and her ears were long and hung down, almost touching her shoulders. She wore a yellow pinny and her green arms bulged menacingly out at the sides. She turned and saw Huron, and her voice softened.

"Ah, Huron, I hope you're not unwell?"

"No, I'm fine. But we have a young one here who has an injured shoulder, and Merlot has hit his head."

She turned and saw Melina.

"I'll look at the young one first," she said, smiling towards Merlot, now realising that he had good reason to be there. "I'll have to ask you two to wait outside."

Huron and Merlot left the room. "Now let's have a look at you," said the nurse. "I'm afraid we're going to have to take your shirt off dear, so we can get a better look at this. If you could stand up?"

Melina stood and the nurse pulled her shirt off gently, easing it over the cuts in her shoulder.

"How did you do this?"

"An eagle attacked me."

"I see, well you've got quite a few nasty cuts there. Did you say an eagle attacked you?"

"Yes," said Melina. It hadn't happened exactly like that, but she did not know how much she should tell her.

"Well, I'm glad to say they are only flesh wounds, nothing too serious. They should heal within a few days."

The nurse skilfully washed Melina's wounds, wrapped her arm in a bandage and then pulled her shirt back over her head, being careful not to move the bandage out of place.

"Now you tell Merlot to bring you back here in two days' time and we'll have another look at it then. Oh, and if you could ask him to come back in I'll take a look at that bruise of his."

"Thank you, I'll tell him," said Melina, getting up out of the chair. She waited outside with Huron whilst Merlot had his wound attended to. Shortly, Merlot reappeared with a bandage wrapped around his head.

"All done," said Merlot. "Now we must go and see the Arrnult. If you feel up to it?"

"Yes, it feels a bit better now it's bandaged."

When they got to the Arrnult's office, Merlot went to see if he was available. He returned looking fed up.

"He's not there, and the guard doesn't know when he's going to return."

An angry voice was raised down the corridor. "I don't care whether he wants to see me or not, I demand an explanation!"

"That is Grunmor," said Huron. "He must not see Melina. Quick Merlot, hide her."

Merlot grabbed hold of Melina's good arm and pulled her into Kurrok's office. They sat down on the floor at the side of Kurrok's desk, out of view of the door. A split second later Grunmor entered the room and saw Huron standing just inside the door.

"Huron, I didn't expect to find you here."

"Nor I you, Grunmor."

"I trust you have important business?"

"All my business is important, Grunmor."

Melina could tell that they didn't get on. She peeked around the corner of the desk. Grunmor was taller than Huron and was dressed in a black hooded cloak with gold trim. She guessed that he was quite old, since his hair was greying and his skin wrinkled. He had a patch of darker skin in the middle of his forehead, which he touched from time to time.

She heard footsteps coming from behind her and pulled her head back in. A door behind them opened and Kurrok walked in. He glanced down at Melina and Merlot and then strode up to greet his visitors.

"Huron, Grunmor, what a pleasant surprise, sit down, sit down," said Kurrok, grasping Huron by the arm and steering him to the chair nearest the side of the desk where Melina and Merlot were hiding. "Now, Huron what is it you needed to see me about?" Kurrok settled into his own chair, comfortable in the knowledge that Grunmor was positioned far enough away not to see Melina or Merlot. "I assume that whatever it is can be said in front of Grunmor?"

"Er... yes, yes of course, I have nothing to hide from Grunmor."

"I have been thinking that er... the gardens outside my window... need... um, tending to, and was wondering... if... if it would be all right for me to approach one of the castle gardeners about it?" asked Huron.

"Yes, of course I would be pleased if you would do so. Is that all?"

"Yes, yes that is all," said Huron, sounding a little embarrassed.

"Right, you may leave," said Kurrok. Huron

made for the door. "Now, Grunmor what is it you wanted?"

Grunmor cleared his throat dramatically. "Hem... It has come to my notice that one of the young ones from the other world has been to visit the Sapphire Crystal Cave."

"Is that so, Grunmor?" said Kurrok a little crossly. He disliked Grunmor's superior manner. "And how exactly did this come to your notice?"

"I heard it from one of the Cullen, who is, I might add, a most reliable source," said Grunmor.

There was a pause, and then Kurrok spoke.

"This is a very serious matter and I shall investigate it personally. If, as you say, one of the young ones has been taken to the Sapphire Crystal, you can rest assured that whoever is responsible will be severely punished. Now is there anything else?"

"No," said Grunmor.

"Good. If you have any more concerns please do not hesitate to come and see me," said Kurrok, escorting Grunmor to the door. He closed the door behind him. "OK, you two, you can come out now, he has gone."

Melina and Merlot got up from behind the desk, Merlot rubbing his posterior.

"That floor is hard, I'm bringing a cushion next time."

"I hope there will not be a next time," said Kurrok.

"Who was that?" asked Melina.

"Oh that, that was Grunmor," said Kurrok, "the leader of the Cullen."

"It sounds like he knows about me visiting the crystal," said Melina.

"Oh, he only suspects it," said Kurrok. "I don't think he knows for sure. You just let me worry about him."

Later when they were all sitting around the fire, Kurrok asked Melina to tell him what had happened at the Great Tower. He sat looking very pleased as she told him how she'd flown, managing to avoid the wall, out over the forest and back again. But when she got to the part with the eagle, his face took on a more worried look.

"That was very brave of you Melina," said Kurrok, after she'd finished. "We have heard that Mydil has a special way with animals, so it is quite possible she sent this eagle to attack you. It is something we will have to bear in mind when we are fighting her. Now I expect you are tired. I have decided that you deserve a rest from your flying lessons, especially with what happened today, so there won't be any tomorrow. Instead, if the weather is fine, you and the others will be allowed out into the castle gardens. Merlot, if you could escort Melina back to her room?"

Melina fell asleep when she got back. She awoke to find that Lisa had joined her.

"Oh you're awake, I was being as quiet as I could," said Lisa.

"I was tired, it must be all the excitement," said Melina.

"What's been happening then? Come on tell me all."

Melina gave Lisa a blow-by-blow account of her afternoon's adventures.

"And you fought this eagle off?"

"Yes."

"That's amazing, I don't know what I'd have done."

"Oh, you'd probably have done the same. It's just what you have to do. You don't have time to think about it."

"How many more flying lessons do you have before you face Mydil?"

"I don't know, I suppose it depends on how fast I learn," said Melina. "Anyway I haven't got any lessons tomorrow, we've all got the day off. We're going into the castle gardens."

"Yes I know, Frydlic told us," said Lisa.

"Food is here!" shouted Merlot, and a tray containing two steaming hot bowls descended slowly towards the floor. Melina hadn't realised how hungry she was until she started eating. She attacked her meal ravenously, finishing it off by licking her bowl.

"I'm tired, I think I'll go to bed," said

Melina rising from her chair. She walked over to her bed and collapsed on top of it. Lisa carried on eating. By the time she'd finished, Melina was fast asleep.

11

"The others are gathered in the hall," said Merlot, as they got to the top of the ladder.

Walking down the stairs, they could hear the other children talking and laughing in the hall below. At the bottom Merlot left them and moved towards the front to join Huron. Melina looked around at the other children. There was Mary, Shaun and Peter, the boy with sensitive hearing (who seemed to have a bit less cotton wool sticking out from his ears than when she'd last seen him) and two girls she hadn't seen before.

"Hi," said a voice behind her. She turned around to see Lenny.

"Oh, it's you," said Melina grumpily.

"Er... yeah. I'm sorry about... well, you know. I hear they're training you to fly," he said, changing the subject quickly.

"Who told you that?" asked Melina.

"Oh, that was me," said Lisa. "Lenny wanted to know why we didn't go back to the Focusing Room that day, and I just had to tell someone."

"Well, I suppose there's no harm done," said Melina, although she wasn't sure if Kurrok would have seen it that way.

"OK, if I could have everyone's attention," shouted Huron, who was now standing at the front, trying to make himself heard above all the noise. "As you all know, you are going to be allowed into the gardens today. The gardens stretch out a long way from the castle itself, so there is the danger that someone outside the castle grounds might see you. We will therefore need to change your appearance so that you blend in."

"What's he mean, change our appearance so we blend in?" asked Lisa.

"Shh," said Melina, "I think he's going to tell us."

"You will therefore be turned into Gamlyns for the day," continued Huron. "Now please don't worry, this has all been done before." He turned towards Merlot. "How many do we have?"

Merlot pulled a roll of paper from his pocket, unrolled it and counted.

"I make it eight."

"Good. They should all fit in easily. Follow me."

He walked across the hall and stopped in front of a large studded door. As the door swung back there were gasps of amazement. The inside of the room was lined with gold. The walls, floor, ceiling; everywhere they looked glistened with gold.

Once they were all inside, the door closed silently behind them and the wall sealed itself, leaving no sign that a door had existed. It was a square room, brightly lit by light shining down from a narrow slit just below the ceiling.

Huron positioned the children in a small group in the middle.

"Please stay exactly where you are," he said, placing a hand on an engraved circular symbol on the wall. A large ring of gold started to move down from the ceiling. It was suspended on golden cords and moved slowly, without making a sound. When it reached about waist height it came to a halt, encircling them. The ring was perfectly smooth and flat, except for a row of large holes along the top. Huron moved his hand to another symbol and a panel nearby opened upwards, revealing two rows of small green figures. He called out to Merlot, "How many girls?"

"Five," said Merlot.

Huron ran his fingers along the figures, selected five, and then walked over and put them into the holes in the ring. By the way he moved around and easily located the holes, Melina could tell that he had done this many times before. The children chattered excitedly, looking at the figures as Huron moved around. Each one was a perfectly carved little Gamlyn girl, as individual as a real Gamlyn. They had little faces, and were dressed in real clothes and finished in great detail. Melina's figure was dressed in a little frilly white top with small black buttons and a light brown ankle length skirt.

Huron returned to the wall, took out three more figures, and placed them into the ring. These were boys, and they were as detailed as the girls.

"Please spread out and stand behind one of the figures in the ring," said Huron. "Girls behind the girl figures, and boys behind the boys."

Once he was happy that they had positioned themselves correctly, he took out a small blue crystal and placed it on top of a gold block inside the panel. He then walked over to the corner of the room and stood next to Merlot.

"Now, please keep absolutely still," he said, moving his hand across onto another panel.

The golden ring began to spin, going slowly at first and then picking up speed, the small Gamlyn figures in the top edge becoming a blur. There was a loud crack as a bolt of blue lightning shot out from the crystal and struck the edge of the ring. In an instant, the ring changed from gold to a vivid blue. Melina stood as still as she was able, holding her breath, in case the very act of breathing should change her position. Bolts of crackling blue lightning leapt across from the ring towards her and she could feel a faint tingling where they touched her. After a while the lightning bolts died away. The ring changed back to gold, and slowed to a halt.

"You can relax again now," said Huron.

Melina raised her eyes and looked at the reflection in the wall. It showed a group of Gamlyn children standing inside a gold ring, but there was no sign of her. Her mind was in a spin, like the ring had been just a few seconds before. And then it struck her. Of course, she was a Gamlyn now. She raised a hand, looking for one of the little green figures to do the same so she could see which of the reflections was hers. Giggling broke out as one by one each of them worked out who was who, and they started to talk in their funny Gamlyn voices. The Gamlyn girl next to her turned towards her.

"Is that you, Melina?" she said in a squeaky voice.

"Lisa... you?" asked Melina, her voice faltering at the shock of hearing herself for the first time.

"Yes, it's me. This is really weird."

Melina looked around for Lenny, and spotted one of the boys dressed in a brown tunic, his bare legs sticking out below. He saw her looking and came towards them.

"Melina?"

"Yes. Is that you, Lenny?"

"Yep."

She looked down.

"Nice legs," she said, giggling. Lenny wasn't amused for a second, but then he saw the funny side and joined in.

"Wow, look at those!" said Lisa.

They turned to look at the figures in the ring, which had now changed to the forms of human children. As they looked closer, they saw that they were exact miniatures of themselves. Lisa reached out to touch one.

"Careful," shouted Huron, "you must not touch those. Merlot, please go and see if the guards are ready."

Whilst Merlot was gone Huron raised the ring back up to the ceiling. He had only just completed the operation when Merlot returned.

"Right, if you would follow me," said Merlot.

Outside the room, they were joined by two of the guards. They followed Huron and Merlot back out of the main door and outside.

Huron led them down a narrow tunnel to one side of the main entrance. The children chattered excitedly in their Gamlyn voices as they followed, their voices reflecting strangely off the walls.

It felt very odd walking along. Their Gamlyn legs were short and stubby, and at one point Melina tripped and had to place a hand on the wall to stop herself from falling. A small wooden door at the end of the tunnel swung back to reveal a sun-lit garden. They crossed a paved area bordered by a low wall and gathered around Huron at the edge of a large lawn.

"The guards have been instructed to be at hand if you need them, so if you get into any bother please call them. Merlot will be back out here later to join you all for a picnic. Any questions? No? Off you go then, but remember – stay within the grounds of the castle."

Melina, Lisa and Lenny left the other children, wandered across the lawn and sat down under the shade of an old tree.

"This is so strange," said Lenny. "I know I'm still me, but I keep looking down and seeing these arms and legs, and I have to keep reminding myself. I mean look at these hands, they're enormous."

"I know," said Melina. "I'm glad there aren't any mirrors out here. So, how's it going in the Focusing Room?"

"I've got two more sessions to go and then I should be back to normal," said Lenny. "Although I think I'm going to miss being able to communicate like that when it's gone. When are you going to be joining us again?"

Melina looked across at Lisa, hoping to get some idea whether she could trust him or not. She thought she could, and told him what Kurrok had told them.

"And this Mydil, she's quite mad?"

"Yes."

"It sounds like it could be quite a fight," said Lenny.

"That's what worries me," said Melina, "I don't think they know how powerful she's become."

They got up to explore the garden. All was very peaceful, with the silence disturbed only by the hum of insects. Ahead of them was a nursery, comprising two big dome-shaped glasshouses with a wide gravel path down the middle. There was a small orchard backing onto the nursery. They followed a rudimentary path between the trees off to one side, where the tall grass had been trampled down.

They hadn't been walking for long when Lenny suddenly yelled out and cupped the back of his head with a hand. He bent down and picked up a large apple.

"Who threw that?" he shouted angrily.

There was a rustling and a foot appeared in the branches of a nearby tree. A Gamlyn boy dropped down from the tree and ran off towards the edge of the orchard. Lenny bolted after him and rugby-tackled him to the ground. But the young Gamlyn hadn't given up, and managed to wriggle free. As he was making his getaway Lenny grabbed hold of his foot and pulled him back down to the ground.

The little Gamlyn continued to struggle underneath him as Lenny worked his way up until he was sitting across the boy's chest. He grabbed hold of the boy's shirt and drew back his fist to punch him.

Lisa looked on horrified. *'No, you mustn't hit him!'* she thought.

Lenny froze and turned around, looking puzzled. He climbed off the Gamlyn, keeping hold of his arm, shook him hard and gave him a piece of his mind before letting him go. The boy ran off and disappeared over a fence at the side of the orchard. Lenny watched him go, brushed himself down, and then wandered back to join Melina and Lisa.

"Little sod. Did you see what he threw at me?"

"I thought you were going to hit him," said Lisa.

"I was, until you stopped me."

"I stopped you?"

"Yes, you called out and asked me not to hit him."

"I didn't call out," said Lisa.

"But I heard you. No, wait. I don't think I did hear you. The words just came into my head. You must have put them there."

"That's impossible," said Lisa. "You're the only one who can do that."

"I know that's how it's supposed to be. But that's what happened."

12

It was getting too hot to sit in the sun, so Merlot had the picnic brought out and placed under the tree they had sat under earlier. And it was quite a picnic. There were long brown loaves of crusty bread; plates of sliced meats; an enormous round pale green cheese with black berries, which only a few of them were brave enough to try, but were glad they did; some round blue fruits with a bumpy skin which tasted like tomatoes; and a mixture of fruit juices in tall clay jugs. And then to top it all off there was a massive pile of orangey jam tarts with a thick creamy topping.

Melina tried a little of everything, even some of the stranger-looking foods. Her taste in food seemed to have changed with her appearance, and she was drawn to food she wouldn't normally touch. She even had some of the tomato fruits, and she didn't usually like tomatoes.

After they had eaten, they stretched out on the grass in the shadow of the tree. Merlot left them again, saying he had something he had to do and would be back later.

Lenny was just dozing off when Melina woke him.

"OK, what are we going to do now?" she asked.

"How about just lazing around here?" said Lenny hopefully.

"No way. Come on, let's see what's over on the other side of the garden. Are you coming Lisa?"

"I suppose so," said Lisa, who had eaten a bit too much at the picnic, and thought lazing around sounded like a great idea.

Skirting the edge of the nursery, they continued further into the garden until they came across a small paved area with a raised pond surrounded by a low grey stone wall. Large red lily pads were floating on top of the water, which was crystal clear. They peered down into the depths, looking for any sign of life. A small yellow fish swam out from under one of the lily pads and swam towards them. It came to the surface near Lisa, blowing a trail of little bubbles. She sat down on the wall and put her hand down into the water nearby and it swam between her fingers.

"This one's really friendly," said Lisa.

After a while it swam away, and disappeared under a lily pad. They continued their exploration of the garden. They came across a little stream and followed it into a small copse. They were quite a way from the castle now, and Melina was beginning to wonder if they'd left the grounds of the castle.

As they emerged from the copse they saw a strange stone building. It was built against a grass bank and constructed of lumps of flint arranged in a haphazard manner, making the walls lumpy and uneven.

"I think it might be a grotto," said Melina, "I've seen them in the grounds of houses back home. Rich people used to build them as a sort of decoration to make their gardens more interesting. They're just there for show really, they don't have any use."

"I think this one might," said Lenny, moving around the front of the stones. "There's an opening here."

It was damp inside and smelt musty and there was green slime growing on the walls. The roof was made of the same stones as the walls and curved over their heads. A few of the stones in the walls had been left out to act as windows, but it was still gloomy inside. There was a narrow alcove at each side, with a stone bench across each one. They ventured further inside and came across a wooden door. Lenny pressed down the latch and pushed, but it was locked.

"Great, a locked door," said Lisa impatiently. "Can we go back now?"

"No," said Lenny sharply. "Look there's daylight coming underneath the door, so there must be a window."

They followed the wall of the grotto to the end where it disappeared into the grass mound.

"Here it is," said Lenny, "behind this bush."

The window was about Gamlyn height and big enough to climb through. It had a broken pane of glass and with the aid of a stick Lenny managed to jimmy it open.

"We're not going in, are we?" asked Lisa.

"Well I am," said Melina, "I want to know what's behind that door."

"Lisa, you stay here and warn us if you hear anyone coming," said Lenny.

"All right," said Lisa, "but don't be long."

"I'll go first," said Lenny. He pulled himself up through the small window, being careful of the broken glass, and dropped down inside. Melina was next. Her Gamlyn arms were strong and she found that she could pull herself up and through the window without much effort. She landed with a thump, her big leather-bound shoes sending up a dust cloud from the mud floor. The room was small and bare apart from a little cupboard next to the window, and what appeared to be a lectern at the other side of the room. There was nothing in the cupboard apart from a long wooden box, which was empty. The box had no markings to indicate what it had once held. They examined the lectern. There were two circular marks on the top, one to each side.

"What do you think made those?" asked Melina.

"Could be cup marks," said Lenny.

"Yes I suppose they could be, but this is a lectern, and only one person would be standing behind it, so why two marks?"

"Good point," said Lenny, impressed by Melina's reasoning.

Melina looked more closely.

"I think they're candlestick marks," said

Melina, "look, there's wax near this one."

They looked around the room for more clues. Melina spotted something on the floor at the base of the lectern, and bent down to pick it up. It was a strip of brown leather with a small, well-worn pocket in the middle. There were two leather strings at each end of the strip, as if to tie it to something.

"What's this?"

"Looks like some sort of sling," said Lenny.

Lisa called from outside, "Hide you two, someone's coming!"

Melina and Lenny quickly dropped down behind the lectern. There were footsteps outside the door and the rattling of a key in the lock. The door opened and someone entered the room, muttering.

"Where is it? I've got to find it," said a male voice.

I wonder what he's looking for? thought Melina. And then she realised with horror that it might be the sling. She had to do something, and fast, or he might come and look for it behind the lectern. She peered around the edge of the lectern and saw a figure with its back to them. Stretching an arm out, she tossed the sling into the corner nearest the door. It landed near the wall without making a sound.

"It's got to be here somewhere," said the voice. He walked towards the lectern, but then stopped and changed direction towards the corner, spotting the sling on the floor.

"Ah there you are. How could I have missed you? Never mind, I have you now."

Melina breathed a sigh of relief.

"Now, the candles," he muttered. He walked over to the little cupboard and opened the door. "Mmm, it's as well I checked. I'll bring more tonight."

With that he walked back out of the room. The key rattled in the lock as he locked the door again. A few moments passed by, and then Lisa called out to them through the window, "He's gone. You can come out now."

Lenny gave Melina a lift up to the window,

and then pulled himself up. Once they were both through he carefully swung the window back and replaced the latch.

"Phew, that was close," said Melina.

"You can say that again. Throwing that sling was sheer genius."

"Thanks. I had to do something or he would have found us. I think that was Grunmor, the Leader of the Cullen."

"Are you sure?" asked Lenny.

"Yes, I recognised his voice, he was in Kurrok's office yesterday."

"It sounds like he's coming back here again tonight," said Lenny.

"Yes, and so are we," said Melina, "we've got to find out what he's doing in there."

"We can't Melina, it's too dangerous," said Lisa. "Anyway we won't be able to get out, the ladder will be pulled up."

"I was thinking about that. I don't think they lock it, so I should be able to fly up and let it down, and then you can climb up it. How about you Lenny, can you get out of your dormitory?"

"Yeah I think so. I'll have to wait for the other two to go off to sleep though."

"What time will that be?"

"It's usually about midnight."

Lisa gave in. "Well all right, but if we're caught just remember it wasn't my idea. Anyway, we'd better be getting back now."

"Yeah, there's nothing else we can do here now," said Lenny.

"Where shall we meet up?" asked Melina, as they walked back towards the castle.

"How about at the bottom of your stairs?" said Lenny.

They arrived back at the lawn and sat down in a circle close to the tree.

"But how will we know when it's midnight?" asked Lisa. "We haven't got any way of telling the time."

"Yes we have," said Lenny. "We can use the Gamlyn clocks. That's as long as you've got one of course. I saw Frydlic looking at the one on the wall in the Focusing Room and he explained it to me. They look like a long plank with writing down the middle."

"Oh yes, I think we've got one of those," said Melina. "It's got a little trolley with a hole in the middle."

"Yeah, that's it," said Lenny, "the hole shows the time. This is what the symbol for midnight looks like."

He drew the symbol on the grass with his finger several times so they knew what to look for, describing it as looking like a figure of eight with a line across the middle. Once it was all settled they joined the other children.

The shadows under the trees were getting longer as it moved into early evening. Only one person didn't look happy and that was Peter, who they soon gathered, had fallen asleep in the sun. His face had gone bright orange, which clashed horribly with the green of the rest of his skin. Shortly, Merlot came back out to join them. He spotted Peter and went straight over to him.

"Oh dear you do not look well," he said

crouching over him. He summoned the guards, and they pulled Peter back onto his feet.

"Take this one to the nurse," said Merlot.

They watched as the guards, with Peter slumped between them, plodded back towards the castle.

"Right, I think it is time to get you all back to normal," said Merlot. "If you would all follow me please."

Huron was waiting for them in the golden room. There was some discussion as to which of the figures was Peter, and then that one was removed and put in the cupboard. The ring whirled around and they were soon back to their old selves again.

13

It wasn't until the girls were in bed that night that they realised there was a slight flaw in their plan. They could read the clock by the light of the orb, but they had no way of knowing when it got to midnight unless someone was watching it.

"Well, one of us will just have to stay awake," said Lisa.

"I'll go first then," said Melina, "and I'll wake you when it's showing halfway to the midnight symbol."

"Sounds good to me," said Lisa, who wasn't

about to argue, since she was half asleep anyway.

Melina sat watching the clock, sitting across her bed with her back against the wall. The little trolley moved slowly up the scale towards the midnight symbol. When Melina thought it was about half way, she got off her bed and walked over to wake Lisa.

"Lisa, it's your turn," she whispered.

Lisa carried on snoring. Melina shook her by the shoulder.

"Lisa!"

"What?" moaned Lisa blearily.

"It's your turn to watch the clock."

"Oh," Lisa yawned. "So I need to wake you when that hole shows that squiggly mark Lenny showed us?"

"Yes, that's it. And stay awake."

"O... K," yawned Lisa.

Melina was asleep almost as soon as her head touched the pillow. She didn't know why, but she surfaced again later and realised something was wrong. There was more snoring coming from Lisa's bed.

"Lisa, wake up," she hissed. She looked up at the clock. The hole had gone past the midnight symbol.

"Lisa, we've got to go."

"Uh."

"We've got to go. You fell asleep," grumbled Melina, trying not to lose her temper.

Melina shook herself awake. Then she flew up and over the wall. She found the rope that operated the ladder, and let it down to Lisa, waiting below. After Lisa had joined her they tiptoed to the door, the orb floating along a few feet above them.

"We've got to do something about that," whispered Lisa pointing to the orb, "it's too bright, someone will see it. Can you make it go darker?"

"I'll try."

Melina concentrated and the orb gradually dimmed.

"I'll leave it like that, any more and we won't be able to see anything at all."

They found the orb hovering above them very disconcerting at first, but as they wound their way down the dark steps they became more used to it, and were glad of its company.

Lenny was at the bottom of the stairs. "About time, I've been here ages," he said gruffly.

"Someone fell asleep," whispered Melina.

"Hmm, sorry," said Lisa, looking sheepish.

Walking as quietly as the stone floor would allow, they made for the main door. Melina and Lenny ordered their orbs to turn off and then Lenny unlocked the door. As he pulled it back it made a loud squeak and they all froze, afraid that someone might have heard it. But luckily no one had, and all was quiet. Lenny gingerly opened the door a little further, making a gap just large enough for them to squeeze through. Then, being aware that there might be guards patrolling the grounds, they cautiously retraced their steps back towards the grotto. It was a clear night, and a pale orange full moon provided enough light to see where they were going.

Arriving at the grotto, they crouched down and moved warily towards the window they had climbed through earlier. There were voices inside and the bush in front of the window was lit by candlelight. The bush gave them good cover, allowing them to see what was happening inside the room without being seen. A small group of Gamlyns in black cloaks were standing in a circle in the middle of the room. They couldn't quite see the whole room, and the lectern was obscured from view by the edge of the window. The Gamlyns were making a strange murmuring sound. Behind the yellow light of the candles was another much brighter blue light, which occasionally flashed across the walls.

The mutterings died away and a single powerful voice spoke out.

"Yes, yes ... "I see the holes... they have grown bigger. And now I see her... but she has changed... she is more powerful."

She is close... much too close. She must be

stopped! We cannot allow her to destroy all that we have achieved."

Melina moved over to get a better view, but lost her footing. She stumbled sideways treading on a stick, which broke with a loud crack.

The voice inside stopped speaking, and the blue light flashed around the room.

"Quickly," whispered Lenny "hide!"

The nearest cover was a bush a little further along the grass bank. But there wasn't enough room for all of them, and Melina was forced to find somewhere else to hide. She ran for the nearest tree at the edge of the copse. Seconds later a Gamlyn man appeared at the entrance to the grotto. As he moved forward the blue light moved with him, sweeping across the ground. The light passed by the bush where Lenny and Lisa were hiding, edging its way towards Melina. A few moments later it settled on the ground to the side of her. Melina froze, with her back pressed hard up against the tree, wishing that she could melt into the bark and disappear. He moved closer. She could hear him breathing. Suddenly, and out of nowhere, a young deer broke the cover of the copse and ran into the opening, crashing through the undergrowth. It stood still, looking at the Gamlyn and then took off again back into the copse.

"Hmm," grunted the Gamlyn, "just a deer."

He turned and walked back towards the grotto. After he'd gone back inside, Lenny and Lisa joined Melina behind the tree.

"Phew, I thought we'd had it that time," whispered Lenny. "Let's get away from here, I don't know about you, but I've seen enough."

"Do you think that was the Cullen in there?" asked Lenny, once they were far enough away not to be heard.

"It could have been," said Melina. "That was Grunmor's voice. But why would they choose to meet out here, in the middle of the night?"

"Maybe this place has special properties, like the ley lines back home," said Lisa.

"Yes, that might be it," said Melina.

"Well I still think it's very strange," said Lenny.

"I tell you what," said Melina, "he'll probably just laugh at me, but I'll ask Kurrok about it tomorrow, after I finish at the tower."

"You can't say we were out here tonight," said Lenny.

"No, I won't. I'll just mention we came across a grotto when we were in the garden, and see what he says."

As they opened the main door they found the orbs hovering exactly where they'd left them. Lenny and Melina thought them to become bright again, and then they returned to their rooms.

14

"*Wake… up.*"

"Uh?" grunted Melina.

"*Wake… up,*" grunted the voice again.

"What's going on?" asked Lisa groggily.

"Someone's calling," said Melina. "Is that you, Merlot?"

"*Yes… you… must come.*"

"But it's the middle of the night," said Melina.

"*I have to take… you… to the place… where… Mydil… was last seen. Come… quickly.*"

After scaling the ladder, they followed Merlot back downstairs to the main door. On reaching the door he waved his hand towards the orbs and they vanished. Melina felt a blast of cold air against her cheek as he swung the door open and she shivered.

They stepped out into the night air. Melina thought she heard the door lock itself again after Merlot had closed it behind them. He quickly set off across the courtyard.

"Where's he taking us?" asked Lisa. "And why is he talking like that?"

"I don't know, but he seems to be in hurry. Come on, or we might lose him."

They went through the archway. At the bottom of the steps on the other side, Merlot stopped and turned towards them.

"Wait here," he whispered, and then disappeared off to one side. He reappeared shortly after carrying a bundle and passed it to Melina. *"Put... these on."*

Melina unravelled the bundle to reveal two long fur coats and passed one to Lisa.

"Now... follow and keep close," whispered Merlot, and set off in the direction of the garden.

He was setting quite a pace and Melina wondered why they were in so much of a hurry. She was feeling wide awake now, even though she'd hardly had any sleep. Turning up the fur collar of her coat, she walked quicker and caught up with Merlot.

"Have we got far to go?"

"Far... not far."

Melina thought he sounded a little strange. Maybe he's tired, she thought and drifted back to talk to Lisa.

"Did he say where we're going?" asked Lisa.

"No, but he said it wasn't far." She looked around to see if she recognised where they were and thought they might be going in the direction of the forest, but she couldn't be sure. They came to a brick wall. Melina guessed from its imposing size that it must mark the boundary of the castle estate. There was a small path that ran alongside it, and Merlot took it without hesitation.

After a while they came to a section of the wall that had crumbled away and Merlot gave a grunt of satisfaction, pleased that he had found what he was looking for.

"Good we go... over," he said.

Although it was now only waist high, it was wide and it took quite some time before they had clambered over it and reached the other side.

"Keep... up," said Merlot, setting off again.

A few feet further on they entered a thicket. Merlot seemed to find it easy to navigate his way through the bushes and Melina wondered whether Gamlyns could see in the dark. They stumbled along, keeping an anxious eye on Merlot, who was getting further in front. The thicket thinned out and they found themselves back out in the open. On and on they walked, following the faint outline of Merlot as he ploughed on regardless.

It seemed to Melina that they must have been

walking for several hours when Merlot stopped abruptly. They caught up with him.

"We shall be going into... the forest soon," whispered Merlot, *"so keep... near."*

"Why does he keep on talking like that?" asked Lisa in a low voice.

"I don't know," whispered Melina, "It's really weird."

Melina could just make out the outline of the trees against the early morning sky as they came to the edge of the forest. A bit further on they saw the glimmer of campfires. There were silhouettes of people around them, and Melina wondered if they were the villagers who had left their homes that Kurrok had told them about.

Merlot didn't appear to notice the campfires, but he seemed to be keeping well away from them, leaving Melina to wonder if he was purposely avoiding them.

After walking on a bit further Merlot stopped and turned towards them. They were in a small clearing.

"We rest… here."

Melina and Lisa sat down on the ground and hugged their knees to keep warm.

"He's acting very strange, have we done something to upset him?" asked Melina.

"I don't think so. Maybe he didn't want to come on this journey. He'd probably prefer to be in bed, I know I would."

The sky was slowly changing to a bluish grey and the trees were taking on a less ominous look as they regained their daytime colours. Melina spotted something high up sitting on one of the branches.

"There's an eagle in that tree."

"What?"

"Over there. That eagle, it's looking down at us," said Melina.

"Do you think it's the same one?"

"It could be. I'd better tell Merlot," said Melina.

Merlot was sitting with his back against a tree at the other side of the clearing, staring at a bush with a faraway look in his eyes and didn't see her come to his side. She moved around in front of him to get his attention.

"Merlot, I think the eagle that attacked us at the tower is in that tree over there."

"*Eagle?*"

"Yes you know, the eagle at the tower."

"*No you are... mistaken.*"

"But Mer..."

"*No!*" he said abruptly. "*Now, we go... on.*" And with that he got up and walked off, disappearing into the forest.

"Lisa, we're moving again," called Melina, following Merlot to make sure she didn't lose the direction he'd taken.

"Did you tell him about the eagle?" asked Lisa as she caught up.

"Yes, he said I was mistaken. I got the feeling he was annoyed that I'd noticed it."

The forest seemed to go on forever and Merlot kept up a fierce pace. They came to the summit of a small hill, and could see from the top that the trees were starting to thin out. Not far away a plume of grey smoke rose from the ground. The mountain that Melina had spotted from the castle was behind it. On reaching the other side of forest Merlot stood still for a few moments, then without looking around, stepped out from under the trees and strode off in the direction of the smoke.

"I suppose he does know we're still here," asked Lisa.

"I don't like this,' said Melina, "he's acting so oddly, and if that's Mydil's camp, why is she making it so easy for us to find her?"

They arrived at the fire. It had been built near a small cluster of rocks and piled high with wet leaves, causing it to belch out thick grey smoke. But it was deserted. Merlot raised a hand towards his mouth and blew through his fingers, making a small chirping sound, then he stopped and listened. A similar chirping sound came from somewhere close by. Without making a sound, two Gamlyn men appeared from nowhere. They were dressed in belted tunics, and carried swords. They both had long straggly hair, and the tallest had a scar down one cheek.

The one with the scar spoke. "You are Merlot?"

"*Yes,*" said Merlot, still in his strange whisper.

"We have been expecting you."

They talked in hushed voices with their backs towards them. Melina looked at the two Gamlyns. She didn't like the look of either of them. They stopped talking and Merlot came over to them.

"*These men... are here... to... guide us. Now, we move... again.*"

"But we're tired," said Lisa.

"*No... we must go.*"

"Can't we rest for a while?"

"*NO... WE MOVE NOW!*" he shouted, and then turned and walked away.

Lisa wiped her eyes and sniffed, forcing back the tears. "He's never been like that before," she said miserably.

"No," said Melina, "that's not like him at all."

One of the guides kicked out the fire and then they set off again. Merlot walked with the taller guide, and Melina and Lisa followed, with the other guide close behind. They were now headed straight for the mountain. As they got nearer the base, the terrain became more barren. The sun lost its battle with the cloud and it started to feel much colder.

Melina looked up and saw the land rising steeply in front. There were narrow tracks in the thinning, wispy grass running from side to side, where an animal had climbed, weaving backwards and forwards to make the going easier. She wondered what sort of animal would choose to live in such a cold, inhospitable place. On and on they trudged, the mountain looming up ahead. The ground became steeper still and they had to use their hands, grasping outcrops of rocks and small clumps of heather to pull themselves up. A fine mist thickened the air and the rocks became more treacherous. The damp clung to their fur coats, forming tiny beads. Melina wondered how far up the mountain they would have to go.

They arrived at a sheer rock face formed by a row of huge flat stones, standing shoulder to shoulder like guards, as if to stop anyone from venturing any further up the mountain. Melina lifted Lisa up so that she could catch hold of the edge of one of the stones. Once she was up, she leaned down over the edge and pulled up Melina. The guide was never far behind, but he didn't seem interested in helping them.

The wind stiffened, buffeting them, and it became harder to make any headway. Every now and again Melina thought she could hear Merlot shouting, but his voice was blown away on the wind. She guessed he was telling them to get a move on. Eventually, after a long climb they saw him up ahead, waiting for them, peering down from a rocky outcrop.

"There you... are," he hissed as they scrabbled up the rock to join him.

Melina walked over to a rock and sat down,

relieved to take the weight off her feet. They were now on a small plateau on the side of the mountain. Ahead all she could see was the edge of the mountain and the stormy-looking sky. She thought about getting up to look around, but decided to rest instead.

"I'm shattered," sighed Lisa, as she slumped down next to her.

"It can't be much further, can it?" said Melina.

"I hope not, I don't think I can do much more of this," said Lisa.

Merlot came over to them. He looked even stranger than before, his face now more orange than green. His eyes were bloodshot, and there was sweat running down his forehead.

"*You must... keep... up!*" he snapped.

Lisa looked up and Melina thought for a second that she was going to protest.

"*The guide has... gone... on... ahead,*" said Merlot and then walked off, disappearing from view. They thought at first that he had fallen off the edge, but on closer inspection saw a small path hugging the side of the mountain. Merlot was cautiously making his way along it. Melina moved further over towards the edge and looked down. They were high up and the view began to swim. Lisa reached out and grabbed her arm.

"Thanks," said Melina, "I was nearly gone then."

The path was narrow and Melina had to make a concerted effort not to look down. Lisa caught up with her. "I hope it doesn't get any narrower," she said.

But as Melina followed the path around the side of the mountain she saw that Lisa's worst fears had come true, as it ended abruptly, and was replaced by a rocky ledge just inches wide. Merlot was waiting at the other side.

"*Keep… your back… against the rock… walk… slowly.*"

"You are joking," said Melina.

"*No! Do as I… say,*" hissed Merlot.

Melina realised that there was no point in

arguing with him and placed a foot on to the ledge. She started to shuffle along sideways, keeping her back against the rock. As she moved along, she could hear small fragments of dislodged rock clattering down the side of the mountain below her. She stopped to steady her nerves.

"*Keep... moving!*" cried Merlot.

She edged forward a few more feet and Merlot reached out, grabbed her hand and steered her to a safe place to stand. She could see in his eyes that he was just going through the motions; there was no feeling in the gesture. She looked away, unable to look at his face, which now showed very few signs of belonging to the Merlot she had once known.

"*Now you... Lisa,*" cried Merlot.

"I don't like this," whimpered Lisa, "I can't do it."

"It's all right Lisa, just move slowly," shouted Melina.

"No, I can't."

"Lisa, you've got to."

"No, no, I can't, I can't," shouted Lisa hysterically.

"MAKE... HER!" shouted Merlot.

The guide drew his sword and moved towards Lisa.

"What's he doing?" cried Melina.

"She will move... now," sneered Merlot. Melina could not believe this was the same kind-hearted Gamlyn who had looked after them in the castle.

The guide moved towards Lisa, threatening her with his sword. "Move!" he snarled, the long scar down one side of his face twisting menacingly.

"Stop him!" screamed Melina. But Merlot ignored her.

"MOVE," shouted the guide again.

"I can't, I'll fall," whimpered Lisa.

He moved nearer. "Move, I will not tell you again," he said, moving his sword closer to her.

Melina watched, horrified, as Lisa tentatively placed one foot and then the other onto the ledge. She shuffled along slowly, keeping her back pressed hard against the rock wall.

"That's it Lisa, just a bit further," called Melina.

Lisa looked across towards her, tears running down her face. Then her foot slipped off the edge. She searched desperately for something to grab hold of but the rock face was almost smooth, and there were no finger holds. Melina could see the fear in her eyes as she slipped down over the edge screaming, "MELINAAAAA!"

Without thinking, Melina leapt off the side. She flew straight down, staying as close to the side of the mountain as she dared. Lisa was tumbling through the air below her. Melina flew fast, faster than she'd ever flown before, pushing the fear and the thought of what would happen if she failed to reach Lisa from her mind. She was only a few feet away from her now. Edging sideways, she stretched out a hand and managed to grab a handful of

Lisa's clothing, but at that moment Lisa rolled away from her, and it was torn from her hand. The ground was coming up fast. She moved closer.

"Lisa, reach out your hand!" shouted Melina at the top of her voice, the air rushing past her and whipping the words away from her mouth.

Somehow Lisa heard her and with a great effort managed to reach out a hand. Melina quickly grabbed hold of it. She hadn't really thought about what she was going to do once she'd got hold of her. She couldn't just fly back up, or Lisa would be pulled from her grip again. The tops of the trees were close. She braced herself hoping that they would break their fall.

15

The sound of splintering wood shattered the peace of the forest as the two girls plummeted down through the tree canopy. After what seemed like an age, they came to a halt. Melina had slowed their fall. It helped that they had fallen into a young tree with springy branches.

"Ow!" said Melina, raising her head slowly from the branch she was lying on. She could see Lisa lying across another branch, below her. She called out to her.

"Lisa?"

Lisa didn't move. She tried again.

"Lisa!"

But still there was no movement.

Melina tried to move her legs, but one foot was wedged in a gap between the branches and she couldn't shift it.

Lisa moaned.

"Lisa, are you all right?"

"Well I wouldn't put it quite like that, said Lisa. How about you?"

"My shoulder hurts and I've got a few cuts and bruises, but otherwise I'm OK. I'm a bit stuck though. Can you climb up here?"

"I'll try."

Lisa's progress was slow because she had to test each branch to make sure it would take her weight, but eventually she reached Melina.

"Which bit's stuck?" she asked.

"It's my left foot. If you grab hold of my leg and pull, I'll wiggle it at the same time, and that might be enough to loosen it."

"OK," said Melina, "pull."

Melina's trainer moved a little way, and then jammed again.

"It moved," said Melina.

"Can't you take it off, asked Lisa?"

"Genius, why didn't I think of that?"

But her enthusiasm soon diminished when she saw that the laces were behind the branch, and there was no way of getting to them.

"No, that's no good. I can't get to the laces. Anyway I always tie them in a double bow."

"Well, we'll just have to pull harder," said Lisa, grabbing hold of Melina's leg again.

"OK. Ready? Pull."

Melina's foot came flying out of the trainer, and Lisa had to quickly grab hold of a branch to stop herself from falling.

Melina grabbed hold of the now empty trainer and twisted backwards and forwards until it came free.

"Right, now what?" asked Melina, putting her trainer back on.

"I don't know about you," said Lisa, "but I

not going back up there, not after that. What's happened to Merlot? He used to be so nice."

"Perhaps it's not Merlot," said Melina, "maybe it's someone who looks like him. But if we don't go back, what are we going to do?"

"I don't know'" said Lisa. "Anyway, we'll have to find a way out of this tree first, and that might be easier said than done."

Some of the branches were a long way apart and they had to dangle perilously, their feet barely touching the branch below, and then with a leap of faith, let go, hoping the branch they had chosen would take their weight. It took a while, but eventually they were both back down on the ground.

"I think we should stay near the edge of the forest," said Melina, "we could get lost in there."

They skirted the edge of the forest, staying under the trees in the hope that they wouldn't be spotted from above. After a little while the ground began to slope downwards, and there was the sound of running water.

"Do you hear that?" said Melina.

"It seems to be coming from over there," said Lisa.

They followed the sound down the hill, although it meant leaving the cover of the trees. There was a small, rock-lined stream running along the bottom. Melina knelt on the bank, scooped up a little of the crystal-clear water in her hands and held it under her nose.

"It smells OK. Oh well, here goes." She took a sip. "It's not bad."

They both drank, gulping the water down until they'd quenched their thirst.

"I'm hungry now," said Melina.

"I may have something," said Lisa, rummaging through her pockets. She found a packet of chewing gum with one stick left. "Here," she said tearing it in half and offering half to Melina. "Better than nothing."

"This is hopeless," said Melina. "I haven't got a clue where we are."

"I was just thinking the same thing. We could always go back the way we came, I suppose. The trouble is, we might bump into Merlot and those other two."

"I think they'll probably come down here to try and find us," said Melina. "What if we hide, and wait for them to go past? And then, after they've gone, we can follow the path back the way we came, back to the castle."

"Well, anything's better than this," said Lisa.

16

After turning back the way they had come, they looked for a hiding place. At first they had no luck, but then Lisa spotted a group of large stones in the distance. As they drew closer they saw the stones formed a ring, which was only broken by a gap about three feet wide on the side furthest away from the forest.

"This looks like a good place," said Melina, as they went through the gap. "Look, there's even a hole here between the stones so we can keep a look out."

The ground inside was mostly mud with the odd patch of grass, and there was a large gap underneath one of the stones. Lisa slumped to the ground and took off one of her trainers. Her foot was bothering her. She pulled her sock off.

"Great," she said, peering at her foot, "blisters. That's all I need." She threw down her trainer and it hit one of the outer stones, making a slapping sound. Melina turned towards where it had landed. Something on it was catching the light. She walked over and picked it up.

"What is it?"

"I saw something twinkling."

"Where?"

"There," said Melina, pointing to the side of the trainer.

"Here, give it to me," said Lisa.

Lisa inspected it. There appeared to be something stuck in the side, near the heel. It caught the light again and sparkled.

"It's a piece of that blue crystal," said Lisa.

"It probably got stuck in there when I slipped over in the cave. It seems to go right through to the inside."

"Of course!" said Melina, excitedly. "That's it."

"What is?"

"You remember that time when Lenny was fighting that Gamlyn boy, and you put that thought into his head?"

"Yeah."

"Well. That's why you were able do it. You must have another power, the power of telepathy, like Lenny, and that crystal made it stronger."

"But how are we going to get it out? I can't walk about with that in there."

"I think you might have to. We haven't got anything to get it out with here."

Lisa lifted her foot and examined it. "That's funny, there's a brown mark where it's been rubbing, and it won't come off."

Melina looked at it and thought she'd seen something like it before, but couldn't remember where. After rubbing her foot for a while, Lisa put her trainer back on. She'd just finished, when there was a loud grunt outside the stones. Melina moved over to the hole and peered through. At first she couldn't see anything because whatever was on the other side was blocking out the light, but then it moved, and she saw the flank of a large animal.

"What is it?" asked Lisa, in a hushed voice.

"It's some sort of animal," whispered Melina. "And it's big."

The animal began to dig, its claws scraping against the stones. After a few minutes digging in the same spot, it moved further around, and began to dig again.

Melina moved over to one side of the gap to stay out of view, and Lisa came to her side. The animal moved and started to dig again. It sounded a lot nearer now, and they could hear it panting. The digging stopped and it snorted. Melina peered around the edge of the gap, and saw a large black paw.

"We've got to do something," whispered Melina. "Quick, put your arms round me and I'll try to fly us out of here."

"No, you can't fly with me on your back. Besides, we might be seen."

A whistle sounded some way off in the distance. At the sound, the creature stopped digging and gave out a long soulful groan. A few minutes passed and all went quiet. Melina crept over to the hole and peered through. She could see a large black bear some distance away, making its way towards the forest.

"It was a bear," whispered Melina. "It's gone now."

She continued to watch until it was swallowed up by the darkness beneath the trees.

"Did you hear that whistle?" asked Lisa.

"Yes, that was odd, it seemed to move away when it heard it."

They leaned back against the stones, grateful for the chance to relax. Melina looked up at the sky. It was still very overcast, and she could only just make out the position of the sun behind the cloud.

"How long do you think we'll have to wait before Merlot goes by?" asked Lisa.

"I don't know. I'm not even sure this is going to work. That bear had us trapped in here, and if Merlot finds us, we'll be trapped again. It's getting too late to make a move today, but I think we'd better head back to the castle in the morn..." She was interrupted by a shrill squawk from above. "It's the eagle! Quick, get under that stone!" shouted Melina.

The gap under the stone wasn't as big as it appeared from the outside and there wasn't much room. Lying on their sides with their knees tucked up, they waited for the eagle to appear. It landed on the stone opposite and stared down at them, craning its neck forward. It sat watching them for a few minutes and then flew away.

They waited a bit longer just to make sure it had gone and then crawled out from under the stone.

"That's funny, I wonder why it didn't attack us," said Melina.

She returned to the task of keeping a lookout for Merlot. After what she guessed must have been a good hour, she decided it was Lisa's turn and turned to tell her. Lisa was fast asleep, her head lolling sideways against the stones. Melina let her sleep and carried on with her watch. There was little to see apart from the grass outside the stones waving gently in the breeze, and she had to fight to stay awake. It became cooler and she was grateful for the fur coat Merlot had given them, and the shelter of the stones.

"I'm hungry," said Lisa suddenly, startling her. "Oh sorry, I didn't mean to make you jump. What are we going to do about food?"

"I don't know," said Melina. "If we were back home we could look for berries or something, but I haven't seen anything out here that looks edible. Besides what's edible at home might not be edible here..."

"Lenny!" blurted out Lisa.

"What?" asked Melina, looking at her friend as if she'd gone mad.

"Lenny. I can hear him."

"What, you mean he's talking to you now?"

"Yes," said Lisa excitedly. "Hang on, I'll try to send him a message back."

Melina watched Lisa's brow wrinkle as she concentrated.

"What's he saying?" asked Melina excitedly.

"He said, he's glad we're OK. He's got some of the guards and Huron's with him. They're coming to rescue us. Huron thinks Mydil is controlling Merlot."

"He thinks we're still with Merlot," said Melina.

Lisa contacted Lenny again and explained how Melina had rescued her, and that they had escaped.

"He wants to know where we are now." said Lisa.

"Tell him we're in a ring of large stones, at the edge of the forest," said Melina.

Lisa communicated the message to Lenny. After a few minutes he contacted her again.

"They know where we are," said Lisa excitedly. "Hang on, something's happened."

"What's happening?" asked Melina.

"I don't know. He just told me to wait a minute."

Lenny made contact again.

"Merlot's just wandered into their camp," said Lisa. "He seems very confused."

"What about the other two Gamlyns?" asked Melina.

Lisa asked the question and then relayed Lenny's reply to Melina.

"They can't get any sense out of Merlot, but there's nobody else with him. And there's more – Huron thinks he was taking us to the Red Crystal Cave."

Suddenly a loud voice boomed out behind them. "Ah, there you are!"

They turned to see Grunmor standing in the gap between the stones, scowling at them.

"Grunmor, you've come to rescue us!" shouted Melina.

"Rescue you? Rescue you?" he cried out incredulously. "No, I haven't come to rescue you. I've come to *kill* you!" he snarled, raising a hand. A bright orange thunderbolt shot out from his fingers and hit the stone at the side of Melina, showering her with fragments of rock. She moved over to one of the lower stones, and started to climb her way out, forgetting in her panic that she could fly.

"Ha, so you run from me," sneered Grunmor. "You are not as powerful as I feared."

Slipping the last few feet to the ground at the other side of the ring, Melina turned and ran towards the woods.

"You are right to be afraid," he shouted. Then he lifted a hand and flew up into the air. He came down several feet in front of her blocking her way, and stopping her in her tracks.

"I shall dispose of you as easily as I would a fly," shouted out Grunmor, and sent another thunderbolt.

But then something strange happened. Before the thunderbolt struck, a green globe materialised around Melina. The thunderbolt hit the globe and then broke up into smaller bolts, which followed a path around the outside of the globe before disappearing into the ground, creating a ring of small explosions around Melina's feet.

Grunmor raised his hand again and sent another thunderbolt, but the green globe appeared again and the same thing happened. He gave an angry scowl, then flew back up into the air and over the stones.

Seconds later there was a cry from Lisa. "Help me, Melina!"

This time Melina remembered to fly. As she landed inside the ring of stones, Grunmor was standing opposite Lisa with his arm outstretched, fingers pointing towards her.

"Now, you will do as I say," he said. "We're going on a little journey, and I am sure I do not need to tell you what will happen to your friend if you do not do as I say."

Melina realised that she was helpless now. With Grunmor behind them, they left the stones and walked back towards the mountain. They hadn't gone far when something flew across the sun, casting a faint shadow on the ground. Melina looked up and saw the eagle hovering in the sky above. It seemed to be following them.

They made their way back up the mountain. About halfway up, they came to an opening in the rock. Grunmor turned towards the eagle, and it flew down, coming to land just above the opening. It twisted its head to one side, looking down at them with cold black eyes. Melina backed a little way down the path. Grunmor saw her discomfort and grinned with satisfaction.

"I have told it to keep watch," he said. "Now come. It will not attack unless I tell it to."

He shoved them both into the opening, and then followed closely behind. They entered a cave. The cave walls were covered in a thick carpet of tiny red crystals. There were more red crystals in the middle, jutting out from the floor, but these were much bigger. There was a smaller tunnel off to one side. Grunmor beckoned Melina towards the far corner, and then, grabbing hold of Lisa's arm, dragged her over to one of the crystals in the middle. He backed her up against it and pulled her arms down by her sides. Then taking a piece of cord from a pocket, he tied her wrists together so that she couldn't escape.

Melina stood watching, feeling helpless and wondering what she could do to stop him. Out of the corner of her eye she spotted a piece of red crystal on the floor near her foot. Feigning tiredness, she slumped down onto the cave floor with her back to the crystal. Then, keeping a wary eye on Grunmor, slowly eased out a hand towards it. She brought it around to her side to examine it more closely. It was the top of a crystal, several inches long and pointed, with a sharp edge at its base. She slid it surreptitiously into the pocket of her coat.

Grunmor finished tying Lisa and turned towards her.

"Now, your turn. Then I can finish this once and for all."

Melina moved towards him. He grabbed hold of her and pulled her towards another crystal next to Lisa, then tied her hands behind it just as he had done with her friend. Once he had finished, he walked towards the back of the cave. He reached into the pocket of his robe and brought out something that Melina had seen before. It was the leather sling that she had seen at the grotto. He looked in another pocket and withdrew a blue crystal about the size of an egg. He placed it in the sling, and then proceeded to tie it around his head. As he was tying it, Melina saw the brown mark in the middle of his forehead. It was the same dark brown as the mark on Lisa's foot.

Keeping her eyes fixed on Grunmor she stretched a hand out towards her pocket and eased out the piece of red crystal. She realised that she would have to get him talking to gain time to cut through the cord.

"So why are you helping Mydil?" asked Melina, rubbing the sharp end of the crystal against the cord.

Grunmor's face darkened as if a storm had passed over it. "Mydil? Mydil?" he bellowed. "She is but a mere puppet!"

Melina thought for a second that she had said the wrong thing, and that now he would kill them both in a fit of rage before she had time to cut through the cord.

"I can conjure up Mydil as easily as this," he said, waving a hand in the air. A swirling white cloud appeared, and then an image of Mydil. The image gave out a cruel cackle of laughter.

"There is your Mydil," sneered Grunmor. "You see? It is I who have the power, not her." He lowered his hand and the image vanished. "Mydil was once of use to me, but I could not control her. She became suspicious and saw what I was planning to do. I found her looking through my notes. She threatened to tell Kurrok, and we fought, but she got away from me. But enough of her. It is I who has tapped into the power of the Sapphire Crystal. It is I who stole this crystal from under the noses of Kurrok and his Seers. It is I who have schemed and planned and have got those other fools of the Cullen to do my bidding. And it is I who shall break through into your world and take from it all that I desire, and then move on to the next. It is I. It is…"

He stopped abruptly, and a thin smile crossed his face.

"But I see what you are doing. You are trying to stall me so your friends can rescue you. But it is too late. You are powerless in here. I, however, with this blue crystal, still have my powers, and with them I shall kill you both."

He raised his arm again.

"Now, you will die!"

At that moment there was a loud growl from the other side of the cave. Standing in the entrance to the cave was the black bear they had seen earlier. It turned its massive head towards Grunmor and fixed him with fearless black eyes. Grunmor stood transfixed, his mouth hanging open. The bear ran towards him, its huge paws pounding across the cave floor. Grunmor ran towards the small tunnel. He was close to it when he slipped and fell, landing heavily on his side. The blue crystal was jolted from the sling and fell to the floor.

The bear growled again and then took a swipe at him, its claws just missing his arm. Grunmor scrambled back to his feet and ran for the safety of the tunnel. The bear tried to follow, but the tunnel was too small for its enormous frame. It stuck its head down the tunnel and growled, then turned back to face Melina and Lisa.

Melina had almost cut through the cord around her wrists, but the remaining thread refused to break. She pulled her wrists apart violently, wincing with the pain as the cord cut into her. The bear came nearer. It got to within a few feet and stood up on its back legs, its head almost touching the roof.

"No, Sheeka!" shouted a voice. They turned to see a young Gamlyn woman standing at the entrance. The bear turned its head, let out a long mournful groan and dropped back down onto all fours.

"There, Sheeka," said the woman, pointing. The bear lumbered over to the far corner and sat down on its hindquarters. The woman came over to Melina and Lisa. She was tall for a Gamlyn, and was wearing a grey stitched fur over one shoulder, with a makeshift rope belt.

"Hello I'm Mydil," she said. "Sorry I had to frighten you, but it was the only way I could think of to stop Grunmor."

Melina looked at her as if she'd seen a ghost.

"But... you're not..." said Melina, her mouth hanging open, unable to finish her sentence.

"Old? No. But I can see why you might think that. I've heard what people are saying about me, and the horrific things I'm supposed to have done. No, I'm only a few years older now than when I managed to escape his evil clutches. Now we must hurry. We cannot let him get away."

She pulled a knife from her belt and cut them both free. The bear was lying on its front now, its chin resting on the floor, looking peaceful.

"Follow me," said Mydil.

They ran towards to the small tunnel, but Melina stopped them just before it.

"Wait – I've got an idea. Help me find Grunmor's blue crystal."

"It's here," said Lisa, finding it close to the wall at the side of the small tunnel.

"Quick give it to me," said Melina.

It was covered in intricate spiral patterns that reminded Melina of the Sapphire Crystal. She could feel its power surging through her.

"OK, I'm ready," said Melina, placing it in her pocket.

17

At the end of the tunnel, they followed Mydil along a narrow twisting path that wound its way up the side of the mountain. The path led to a plateau. As they climbed up onto it there were several large explosions, forcing them to take cover behind a nearby cluster of rocks.

Melina looked between the rocks. The guards had taken refuge behind a long rocky outcrop at the other side of the plateau, and Grunmor was attacking them with thunderbolts. There were several large craters along the front of the rocks, and the middle section had crumbled away.

Lenny appeared at the far end of the outcrop clutching a sword. He was creeping slowly towards Grunmor, who was facing the other way, watching the guards at the other end of the rocks. The guards were creating a noisy diversion, striking the ground with the handles of their spears, and shouting. Lenny looked scared, and Melina could see that his sword hand was shaking. Grunmor swung around to face him.

"You fools, these toys cannot harm me," he snapped. He pointed at Lenny's sword and it began to swing upwards. Lenny grasped hold of it with both hands, trying to force it back down, but the sword continued its unstoppable journey, tilting up towards the sky. Lenny's feet left the ground. He quickly gained height, dangling precariously above the plateau, his body twisting, as he tried in vain to wrestle his sword from the magical grip Grunmor had placed upon it.

Melina looked on horrified. Surely he couldn't hang on forever? She was about to shout out to him, to tell him to let go, when he dropped back down onto the plateau, landing heavily, and toppling forwards onto his hands.

Grunmor waved a hand at the sword and it disappeared over the edge of the plateau.

"And now you will join your sword," he snarled, taking several steps towards him. He raised a hand and threw a thunderbolt at Lenny. But Lenny, having got back to his feet, managed to leap out of the way and it struck the ground, blasting a large crater where he'd been standing.

Melina had seen enough. She jumped to her feet and ran across the plateau towards them.

"It's me you want. Let them go!" she shouted.

Grunmor turned to face her. "So you still think you can challenge me, a mere slip of a girl?" he snarled. He turned back towards Lenny and raised his hand again. But before he could send another bolt, there was a loud rumbling and the ground shook violently. A crack appeared, which quickly spread towards the edge of the plateau, and the ground under Lenny gave way.

"LENNY!" shouted Melina. But it was too late. He was gone.

She took to the air, flying over towards where he'd fallen, but Grunmor anticipated her move and flew up in front of her, blocking her way. Melina flew away from him. She was crying, tears streaming down her face, as she thought of how ruthlessly he had disposed of her friend. She wiped the tears away with the sleeve of her coat, and then came back around towards him, with her fists together and out in front of her, ready to strike him.

Grunmor let her get close to him. Then, at the last minute he dodged out of the way. As she flew past he reached out and grabbed hold of her ankle and swung her back around, holding her fast around the middle.

"You have been enough trouble to me!" he snarled.

He was strong, and could easily hold her

with one arm. He squeezed harder. She could hardly breathe, and knew she had to do something, and quickly. She kicked down hard, scraping the heel of her trainer down his shin. He screamed out, at the same time relaxing his grip. She took a deep breath, and then shouted out to Lisa, "Lisa, use your fire!"

Lisa raised a hand and blue sparks leapt from her fingertips. They shot across the sky, missing Grunmor by several feet. She tried again, and this time struck home, hitting him squarely between the shoulder blades. Grunmor let out a yell and let go of Melina. Melina seized her chance, and flew away from him at great speed.

Grunmor grimaced, and sent a thunderbolt streaking across the sky after her. Melina dodged it, and it hit the ground a few seconds later in a great ball of orange flame. He sent another much larger thunderbolt, which screamed across the sky, as if the sky itself was being torn apart, lighting up the plateau in a fiery red glow. The speed of it surprised her. It was upon her before she knew what was happening, and was about to hit her when, the green globe appeared around her. The bolt smashed into the globe, sending out a mass of bright green and orange flame, then split in two, passing around each side of the globe, leaving Melina stunned, but unharmed inside. Grunmor scowled; annoyed by the apparent ease with which she survived his attacks.

Melina had begun to realise the true might of Grunmor's power. But she also realised that for her plan to succeed, she would need to get near him.

Sliding a hand into her pocket, she pulled out the piece of red crystal she'd picked up from the cave floor. As she took hold of it she felt her power weaken, and quickly grabbed hold of Grunmor's blue crystal with her other hand.

Grunmor had turned his attentions to Lisa, and was now hovering above her at the other side of the plateau. He sent a thunderbolt into the rock she was hiding behind, blasting a hole in it.

"The next one will see the end of your friend, if you do not stop this foolishness," raged Grunmor. "You know I am stronger than you, and that I will win in the end."

Melina flew slowly back towards him, clutching the red crystal tightly in her fist, with her other hand around the piece of blue crystal in her pocket. Just a bit closer, she thought...

"Ah, so you see that you cannot defeat me," said Grunmor, grinning smugly as she approached him. He reached out to grab hold of her. In an instant Melina flew up and over the top of him, forcing the red crystal down into the folds of his hood. Grunmor let out a cry, realising what she had done. With his powers removed, he could no longer fly. He went hurtling downwards, his arms thrashing about as he tried desperately to remove the crystal. She turned away, knowing what his fate must be, and flew back towards the mountain. She landed on the plateau next to Lisa and Mydil.

"Are you hurt?" asked Lisa.

"No, but if you hadn't helped, it would have been quite a different story."

"You put up quite a fight up there," said Mydil. "You're tougher than you look."

"Thanks," said Melina, "it was touch and go there for a while. I wasn't sure if I would be able to get close enough to use the red crystal without him getting hold of me again."

A faint voice called out. "Help, can anybody hear me?"

It was coming from the edge of the plateau. They rushed over and peered down. Lenny was standing on a small ledge below them.

"Lenny, you're alive!" cried Melina.

"Just about," said Lenny, "I hit my head. I was out for a while. What happened to Grunmor?"

"He fell," said Lisa, making a gesture with the side of her hand across her throat.

"Good riddance," said Lenny. "There's just

one problem now, and that's how do I get back up there?"

"I think I might be able to help there," said Mydil. "I've got some rope hidden not far from here. If you can just hang on a little longer, I'll fetch it."

The guards, seeing that Grunmor had been beaten, came out from behind the rocks to join them.

After a short time Mydil returned with a rope coiled over her shoulder. She lowered an end down to Lenny and he tied it around his waist. The guards pulled on the rope, and with Lenny kicking against the rock to keep himself away from the side, they hauled him back up.

Mydil turned towards Melina and Lisa. "Listen, I must be going," she said.

"But why?" said Melina. "Surely now Grunmor's gone you can come back to the castle?"

"No, I won't be coming back. I like it out here, especially now I have Sheeka. I couldn't take him back there. No, I'm happier here."

"Well, I'll tell Kurrok what you've done for us," said Melina, "and thank you."

"Yes thanks," said Lisa, "and good luck."

"Who was that?" asked Lenny, after Mydil had gone.

"Oh, that," said Melina. "That was Mydil."

It was too far for them to walk back to the castle that day, as it was already getting dark, so they made camp. The guards had brought blankets for them, and as they lay beneath the stars, the full extent of what had happened that day slowly began to sink in.

"But what happened to Merlot?" asked Melina. "Is he all right?"

"I hope so, he looked awful," said Lenny, "and he was so confused. We thought it was best to get him back to castle so the nurse could have a look at him. Huron went with him."

18

After a night's uninterrupted sleep, Melina was starting to feel more like her old self again. Lisa and Lenny were already up and talking to the guards, who were busy cooking breakfast over an open fire. She walked over to join them.

"We were trying not to wake you," said Lisa. "You were sleeping so solidly. Look, Lenny's got the crystal out." She passed the small shard of blue crystal to Melina. "Careful, it's sharp."

"We'd better take this back and give it to

Kurrok, for safe keeping." said Melina. Taking her handkerchief out, she wrapped the little piece of crystal inside, folding in the ends carefully so it couldn't fall out, and then put it back in her pocket.

After breakfast, they rolled up their blankets and headed back to the castle. They had been walking for some time when Melina spotted the eagle again, sitting in one of the trees. It came down and landed nearby.

"No," cried Melina, backing away from it, "get away from me!"

The guards rushed to her aid, standing between her and the eagle, hands on the hilts of their swords.

"It's just sitting there," said Melina, after a while.

"Maybe now Grunmor's dead it's not evil any more," said Lenny.

Melina looked at it more closely. "It does seem less threatening than before," she said.

A second eagle flew down and the two rubbed beaks.

"I wonder if that one's its mate?" said Lisa.

The eagles took to the air, spiralling around and slowly gaining height, before disappearing from view over the treetops.

When they got back to the castle the guards made sure they were safely inside before saying goodbye and going back to their quarters. Kurrok and Huron were there to greet them in the hallway.

"Oh, it's so good to see you all again. Come this way, come this way," said Kurrok, leading them into his office. Sitting down in front of a roaring fire, they relayed to Kurrok what had been happening.

"And Grunmor, you saw him fall?"

"Yes," said Melina. "Oh, before I forget, here's the crystal he was using," she added, taking it from her pocket and handing it to him.

Kurrok held it up to the light, turning it around and marvelling at the intricate patterns carved into its surface.

"I can see now why he was so powerful," said Kurrok. "Huron, please take this, and find out how he was using it. Once we know that, we should have a better idea of how to seal those holes."

"Of course," said Huron, taking the crystal.

"And you say Mydil is still young?" said Kurrok after Huron had gone.

"Yes, and she is completely innocent," said Melina.

"We wouldn't be here now, if it wasn't for her," said Lisa.

"I shall see to it personally that her name is cleared, and she will be allowed back into the castle any time she wishes," said Kurrok.

Once he'd heard all they had to tell, he leant back in his chair and gave out a long sigh.

"But there's one thing that still puzzles me," said Melina.

"Yes?" said Kurrok. "Please ask me anything, anything at all."

"Did you suspect the Cullen were involved in all this from the beginning?"

"Well, not exactly. You see we had been trying to capture Mydil for some time. But on each occasion, just as we were about to put the final part of our plan into action, she would somehow manage to escape. It was as if she was one step ahead of us all the time. I wondered if she had found some way of seeing into the Cullen, and so decided to keep our plans from them.

"Shortly after that, Huron spotted you, and we realised that you would be the one to help us. It was all going to plan until you both went missing. After that I summoned Huron and he told me how you were friends with Lenny. We asked Lenny to help us. He told us about the incident in the garden, and we hatched a plan to rescue you. Lenny's power was dwindling, so he was taken to the Sapphire Crystal. And the rest you know. We are indebted to you all. Now, I really must get on, and you should visit Merlot."

"Hello Melina," said the nurse, bumping into them in the corridor.

"We've come to visit Merlot," said Melina. "How is he?"

"He seems to be recovering slowly. Come, I'll take you to him."

They followed the nurse down a corridor into a small ward to find Merlot propped up on pillows in a bed next to a window.

"Merlot, you have some visitors," said the nurse. "Now, I need to check that wound Melina, so please look in at the office before you go. Oh, and don't stay too long, he tires easily."

"OK," said Melina. She turned to Merlot. "Hello Merlot," she said softly. "How are you feeling?"

Merlot turned his head slowly towards her. His face was pale and he looked vague and distant. He was looking a slightly better colour than the last time she had seen him, but his eyes were still bloodshot.

"Merlot, it's us. Melina, Lisa and Lenny."

"Me... lina," said Merlot slowly in a hushed voice. "Melina... Lisa... round... room," he added, looking pleased that he could remember.

"Yes, Merlot, that's right, we're in the round room."

"Grunmor!" said Merlot, struggling to sit up, and looking frightened.

"It's all right Merlot, Grunmor is dead," said Melina.

"But I was... taking you to him."

"It's all right Merlot, we know," said Lisa.

"Now, you rest and get better, there is nothing to worry about now," said Melina.

"He looks so tired," said Lenny as they left the room.

"Yes, poor Merlot," said Melina.

Melina went to see the nurse, and she put a fresh bandage around her shoulder. Her injury was mending nicely, and the nurse told her that after a few more days it wouldn't need a bandage.

It was back to the Focusing Room for Melina, Lisa and Lenny. Mary was missing, and Frydlic told them that she'd had her powers removed and had been returned home. They visited Merlot each day over the following week, and as he slowly recovered they told him what had happened in the mountain, and how Grunmor had been defeated.

"Wake up please."

Melina opened her eyes and squinted up towards the roof. She could see a familiar face peering down at her over the wall.

"Merlot!" shouted Melina. She quickly climbed up the ladder to meet him, followed by Lisa. "Oh Merlot it's good to see you looking so well again."

"Yeah, it's great," said Lisa.

"Thank you," said Merlot, his face going purple, as he was a little embarrassed by all the attention. "Now, I'm to take you to see the Arrnult, he has something important to tell you."

Huron and Lenny were sitting in Kurrok's office, and the door was open.

"Ah, there you are," said Kurrok, spotting them at the door. "I have some good news."

They walked into the office and sat down next to Huron and Lenny in front of Kurrok's large opulent wooden desk.

"Huron has been looking at what Grunmor was up to," said Kurrok, "and I am happy to say that he has made great progress. Huron, if you would be so kind?"

Huron cleared his throat. "As we now know, Grunmor was controlling Merlot's mind so that he could use him to take you to the Red Crystal Cave. However, it seems Merlot was not the only one he was controlling. He was also controlling other Gamlyns. Several senior members of the Cullen have similar symptoms to Merlot, and have only a vague recollection of what has been happening. Fortunately, without Grunmor's influence they will recover, although this may take some time.

"The smaller crystal was the key to his power. He had linked the power of the Sapphire Crystal to it, linking this in turn with his own mind. You did well to separate it from him, as with it he was unstoppable. Now that I understand the link between the two crystals, I should be able to undo the damage he has done and close the holes in the fabric of space between our worlds."

"Huron has also made another important discovery," said Kurrok. "It seems the orbs the Cullen gave us were not the gift we thought they were. Grunmor was using them to spy on us. Watching our every move. Through them he could see what we were planning to do, and then use that information to outmanoeuvre us. It was how he managed to stay one jump ahead of us all the time, and stop us from discovering that he was the one who was plotting against us."

"I thought there was something strange about those things," said Lisa.

"But that is not the most important news," said Kurrok. "The news, which I'm sure you will be overjoyed to hear, is that Frydlic has informed me that your powers have been removed, so it is now safe to return you back to your world."

Up until that moment Melina hadn't realised how homesick she was. She had missed them all so much, even Joe, which came as a bit of a surprise.

"When are you sending us back?" asked Melina.

"Tomorrow morning," said Kurrok.

"Do you hear that Lisa? We're going home, were going home!" sang Melina, grabbing hold of Lisa and swinging her around in a little dance.

Lenny didn't look quite so thrilled.

"Come on Lenny, smile, we're going home!" said Melina.

"Yeah, it's great news," said Lenny. "But I'm going to miss all this."

"Yeah, me too," said Lisa.

"Ah," said Kurrok, "That will not be so. You see, we cannot allow you take back any knowledge of this world. So as you travel back, memories of this world, and all things connected with it, will be removed. I'm sorry to say that you will not remember any of this."

Nobody spoke for a minute, each of them with their own thoughts. Melina broke the silence.

"So, how long have we been gone? I mean, I know it's been two weeks here, but I remember you saying that there was some sort of time difference between our worlds."

"Ah yes. Huron, do you have any figures to hand?"

"Yes. If we send you back tomorrow as planned, the time that will have passed in your world will be about three days."

Melina's mind drifted to thoughts of home. What would be happening there? Joe's birthday had been about a week away when she'd left, so she hadn't missed it. She still had time to buy him a present.

****

The next day, Melina and Lisa accompanied

Merlot down the stairs for the last time. As they came down the steps and through the archway, the cart was waiting for them, with Kurrok, Huron and Lenny standing nearby.

Kurrok shook Melina firmly by the hand. "Goodbye, and thank you once again."

Melina gave Merlot a big hug. "Bye Merlot, and thanks for everything."

After saying their farewells, they climbed up into the cart and sat down.

****

Melina sat up against the headboard and rubbed her eyes. She was surfacing from a deep sleep, and she felt quite fuzzy-headed She pulled back the curtain. Outside it was early morning, and spitting with rain. She climbed out of bed.

As she sat on the end of the bed brushing her hair, she felt something dig into her thigh. Sliding a hand inside her pocket, she pulled out her handkerchief. It had been folded into a neat parcel, and there appeared to be something inside it, as she could see a small, hard lump in the middle. She placed it on the bed beside her and unfolded it, but couldn't see anything. She folded it up again, and the lump reappeared. That was *odd*. She re-opened it and gently brushed her fingers across the surface. As they reached the middle, they touched something hard and sharp...

At that moment, in a flash, all her memories of the Gamlyn world came flooding back to her. Of course – the shard of blue crystal which she had meant to hand over to Kurrok. She still had it, but it was now invisible. And touching it had brought back the memories which the Gamlyns had tried to erase.

Melina folded the invisible piece of crystal back inside the handkerchief and placed it inside a wooden box on top of the chest of drawers for safe keeping. Then she opened the bedroom door. She could hear the familiar sound of the radio downstairs. She ran down to find her mother sitting at the kitchen table. Melina ran up behind her and threw her arms around her, making her jump and spilling her coffee.

"Oh Melina, it's you," she said, half-turning around. "You gave me quite a fright. You're up early. Now, what are you having for breakfast? Are you seeing Lisa today?"

She was home.

Just published by Mereo:
The Lost Shard – a thrilling sequel to The Sapphire Crystal

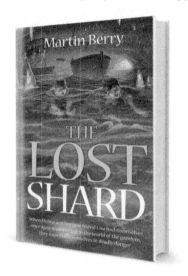

By the same author: *Glow Worms*

Printed in Great Britain
by Amazon

33941646R00136